UNDER THE OLD OAKS

MAX STOOD A LITTLE APART, DRINKING IN, WITH ALL THE FORCE
OF HIS NATURE, THE GLORIES OF THE SCENE   Page 51

UNDER THE OLD OAKS

BY

E. EVERETT GREEN

Author of "His Mother's Book," etc.

EXCELSIOR LIBRARY

PICKERING & INGLIS
LONDON GLASGOW EDINBURGH

London: 14 Paternoster Row, E.C.4
Glasgow: 229 Bothwell Street, C.2
Edinburgh: 29 George IV Bridge

THE EXCELSIOR LIBRARY

19 THE LADY OF HERON'S COURT..E. E. Enock

20 AILEEN ....L. Barter Snow

21 CONCERNING JENNIFER.........B. J. C. Harris

22 NANCY ELLERTON.................Nora C. Usher

23 OPENED DOORS....................Brenda

24 GRAFTON DAYS.....................K. M. MacLeod

25 THE FORGOTTEN SON............Grace Pettman

26 BLINKS ....S. E. Burrow

27 UNDER THE OLD OAKS.........E. E. Green

28 TRUE AS STEEL ....S. E. Burrow

29 NOODLE..............................S. E. Burrow

Made and Printed in Great Britain

CONTENTS

—•—

I. Oakwood Castle 7

II. The Young Bride 17

III. The Motherless Children 30

IV. The Waterfall 44

V. The Soldier's Farewell 56

VI. The Young Musician 64

VII. The Cottage in the Glen 71

VIII. Little Gretchen's Mission 83

IX. The Secret Disclosed 91

X. The Baby Girl 97

XI. Cousin Karl 105

XII. Gretchen's Class 112

XIII. Eventide 119

XIV. Farewell to Oakwood Castle 127

ILLUSTRATIONS

MAX STOOD A LITTLE APART DRINK-
ING IN THE GLORIES OF THE
SCENE, ... *Frontispiece*

FACING PAGE

"THIS IS MY ELDEST AND ONLY
GRANDSON," SAID THE STATELY
OLD LADY, ... 32

"WHAT IS THE MATTER TO-DAY,
LITTLE WOMAN?" MR. OGILVIE SAID
KINDLY, ... 80

UNDER THE OLD OAKS.

CHAPTER I.

OAKWOOD CASTLE.

" Where the long trembling ivy spray
   Half hid the centuries' decay,
   In solitude and silence grand
   The castle towered above the land."

RE you sure they will come soon, Aunt
Hannah ? "

" Of whom are you talking, Gretchen ? "

" Oh, aunt, you know ; why, of Uncle
Jack and his bride. Grandmamma said
she expected them ere long ; but when, I wonder ? "

The questioner was a little girl, who lay on a
couch in a small old-fashioned parlour in a castle
in one of the southern counties of Scotland. The
very fact of her lying as she did proved she was
an invalid, for the time we write of was in the
early part of the present century, when easy

couches and luxurious chairs were less commonly used than they are now-a-days. Certainly the lady whom the child addressed as aunt would have scorned the idea of lolling back on sofa or chair, bolt upright she sat, book in hand, apparently engaged in some deep study, from which she did not wish her attention to be diverted.

But the child was in a talkative humour, and more disposed than was her usual way to question the stiff aunt she decidedly feared. A few moments' silence, then she spoke again :—

"Isn't Edith a pretty name? Do you think you will like her, Aunt Hannah?"

The lady, forced to reply, looked up with a worried air. "It is hardly likely," she replied, "that a girl of seventeen years and I should have much in common. What can have induced Jack to marry a child, I can't imagine; a pretty doll's face, I daresay, will have been her chief attraction."

The speaker (herself on the shady side of forty) was somewhat annoyed by the little girl's joyous tone, as she said, "Oh, is Aunt Edith so young? then I *am* glad, very glad! for, except Max, I never see any young person; every one in this castle is old,—grandmamma, papa, you, and all the servants; oh, I am so glad the new aunt is young! Will she like me, I wonder?"

This last remark was said in an undertone, hardly meant to reach Aunt Hannah's ears; but it did nevertheless, and that lady, who had felt not a little nettled at being classed by the child in the list of old people, replied sharply, "It is most improbable that she will, Gretchen, unless you learn to control your temper better, and seek to make fewer impertinent remarks. No one can love you as you now are."

The child's large dreamy blue eyes filled with tears, and she said quietly, "I know; but sometimes the pain is so bad. I can't help being cross, and I do weary lying here all day. But," she added after a pause, "papa *does* love me a little, and Max does a great deal, and so I am sure do the old oaks."

"'The old oaks!' Gretchen, really you are too absurd; you forget you are eleven years old now, and should be ashamed of continuing your childish fancies about these old trees. 'Pon my word, to hear you talk, one would fear you were an imbecile."

Poor little motherless Gretchen! she had a strange life of it in that queer old castle, every nook and cranny of which spoke of days gone by, whilst the dilapidated appearance of many of its rooms, and even of the once beautiful towers, told

of fallen fortunes, and of pride and poverty com-
bined. The family still kept up, or tried to keep
up, a certain state ; an old man acted as butler,
and some faithful old women-servants helped to
keep up the appearance of the past.

Gretchen's father, Mr. Ogilvie, was the Laird of
Oakwood Castle; a widowed and gloomy man, yet
hiding, under a proud, reserved manner, a true
loving heart. And few knew how deeply he had
suffered when, nine years before the time we write
of, his gentle German wife had died whilst on a
visit to her father's house, leaving two young
children,—Max then being four years old, and
fair-haired Gretchen a little maiden of two. From
the time of her death, the laird (as he was always
called) had resided entirely at Oakwood Castle, his
mother and sister living with him, and nominally
bringing up the orphan children. Old Mrs. Ogilvie, a stiff, proud, stately lady, was more feared
than loved by her own children, and dreaded by
her grandchildren. In her presence little Gretch-
en's words were few—indeed, her grandmamma
had early taught her that children should never
speak to their elders unless spoken to ; and even
Max, of whom in her own way the old lady was
proud, hardly dared to speak in her presence.
Very rarely did Gretchen venture to question any

one, or make remarks of her own, as she had done to Aunt Hannah the day our story begins. Suffering, often greatly, from disease of the hip-joint, which kept her quite confined to the sofa, she often became irritable. Poor child, in all that household there was not one hand gentle enough to soothe her, and pity rather than severely blame her for fits of temper. Sometimes the father longed to take the suffering child into his arms, and caress her, as he knew her own gentle mother would have done; and once (and Gretchen never forgot the day), when she was in greater pain than usual, he knelt beside her couch, and tenderly drawing her to his breast, kissed her forehead, saying, "Dear little Gretchen, would I could ease you, my child!" But at that moment his mother entered the room, and he rose quickly, knowing well he would draw down on his head a severe reproof for spoiling the child. And man as he was, he feared still the mother whose word was law to all around her.

But in every lot there is compensation for all trials, and Gretchen had some pleasures of her own. One was her intense love for, and pride in, her young brother Max. How he loved that helpless little sister! On her the whole deep affections of his nature were centred, and reproof, and even punishment, did not prevent him from devoting himself to her. And again and again the boy thanked God (though to him an almost unknown God), who had given him a gift which in Gretchen's most wayward moments could calm and please her; for Max inherited from his mother a marvellous talent for music. Often in the still twilight hours, through the old castle would sound the rich, full notes of the organ, played with a touch and taste that one could scarcely believe came from a child's hand. At such times Gretchen's greatest joy was to watch her brother as he sat wrapped in delight, his large gray eyes full of enthusiasm, and his whole spirit engrossed in the beautiful thoughts which he seemed to bring out of the organ. And sometimes he would raise his voice in singing some Scottish psalm to one of the grand old tunes that had again and again been sung on the sides and summits of the hills that surrounded the old castle, in days when the only places where many of our forefathers could worship God in the way which they thought best was on hill-tops and in woods; and even there, times without number there were when

> " The melody died 'mid derision and laughter,
> As the host of ungodly rushed on to the slaughter."

Dearly did both the children like to read or hear

stories of those days; and on the long summer evenings, when they were alone, Max would draw little Gretchen's couch close to the window, and point out to her the different hills on the tops of which (old Thomas the butler told him) the Covenanters, in days gone by, posted men to look out for their enemies, and give timely warning to the little band of praying ones who were met together to worship God. Often, whilst the boy thus spoke, the sun would drop down behind the hills, and a purple haze envelop them in a beautiful mantle. The children dearly loved those hills, and their stirring imaginative minds fancied them as still peopled with persecuted men and women, or more certainly with the "brownies," of which the country people delighted to talk, and stories of which old Thomas and Betty Johnston (the so-called housekeeper) on the long winter evenings would tell the children in the nursery, when the old lady and the laird and Miss Hannah were occupied playing cards in the sitting-room.

Yet, though the children had from infancy thus heard tales of those who loved to meet together to pray and praise, of the real God, of the loving Saviour to whom they prayed and in whom they trusted, they knew nothing   A form of prayer, it is true, rose from their lips morn and eve; but

they had never been taught to look up to and love
the One to whom it was addressed. In that old
castle *form* had taken the place of the living God.
Yet sometimes, as Max was playing dreamily on
the organ, a dim remembrance would fill his mind
of soft blue eyes bending over him, and one speak
ing to him words of holy love, in which the name
of Jesus mingled; and at those times his heart
was involuntarily raised to heaven, and the chords
he struck, so full of melody and reverence, were
indeed the utterance of a soul seeking after the
true God.

To his grave, stern father, Max was a sore perplexity; the boy was studious and quick at his
books, but his heart was not in them. A strange,
dreamy boy he was, his whole soul absorbed in
harmonious sounds. Inheriting in some degree
the gravity of his father, his words were few;
indeed, the natural gaiety of childhood had been
early checked by his upbringing. His tutor, an
old man who had educated his father, had been
heard to say that Master Max poured out all his
thoughts only through the organ. "'Twas a thousand pities," said his Aunt Hannah, "that that
organ had been brought to the castle; if it had
not been, Max would not have wasted so much
of his time making a noise on it." The latter

remark had been made more than once in the boy's
presence, and had set a flush of indignation over
his countenance, but the strict discipline enforced
by every member of the family obliged him to
force back the angry words that rose to his lips;
then ere long the organ would be heard uttering
as clearly as speech could have done the story of
the boy's grief and indignation. And little Gretchen understood it all, and quietly said, "Never
mind, Max, you and I know all about it, and so
do——" Here she would pause and shake her head
mysteriously, and whisper low, as if afraid of being
overheard, "The old oaks; don't they, Max?"

So questioned, Max would sit silent for a few
moments, lost in thought. Of course, he knew he
ought to tell his little sister that the old oaks could
know nothing about it, that it was childish in her
to think so; but he could not find it in his heart
to take from her a delusion which gave her such
intense pleasure, so he too nodded his head wisely,
and said, "Who knows, Gretchen; they are very,
very old and wise-looking, these wonderful old oaks.
Oh, I shouldn't wonder they know all about us,
and could tell us strange stories about many things.
Little sister, do you know they must have seen
mamma? she lived here once for some months. I
wish they could speak,—don't you?"

Gretchen looked more mysterious than ever. "They do," she said, "to *me often*."

"Oh, Gretchen, when?"

"On summer days, when I lie under their shady branches; they do speak to me then. Max, you need not laugh; they speak to me, and love me, and are so good to me. Oh, I do love them! but nobody believes me, not even you, Max, so I'll say no more about it."

Yes, the suffering child found one of her greatest pleasures in the companionship of the old oaks. To her they did indeed speak, as all inanimate nature does speak to thoughtful minds; and I am not sure they had not conveyed messages to little Gretchen of the love and tenderness of the good God who had created her and them : in one sense surely trees and flowers, and all God's works, preach of him. What if little, untaught, fanciful Gretchen confused and intermixed these messages and her fancies together, and refused to separate the one from the other. Pity she could not have known Michelet. I rather think the great historian and the dreamy thoughtful child would have understood each other, and would have spent some delightful hours together under the old oaks!

CHAPTER II.

THE YOUNG BRIDE.

"And her smile it seemed half holy,
As if drawn from thoughts more far
Than our common jestings are."

THESE old oaks were very wonderful ones, and ere we proceed with our story, in which they bear a part, we must endeavour to tell our readers something about them; and as they still exist, should any be desirous of visiting them, they can easily find out their whereabouts and judge for themselves if our account of them be true or not, only bearing in remembrance that

"The eye sees all around, in gloom or glow,
Hues of its own, fresh borrowed from the heart."

The season we write of, when the newly-married couple were expected at Oakwood Castle, was early summer. June had not yet merged into July, and nature was still clad in its freshest, brightest green. The old oaks were looking their very best as the sunbeams glinted down through their leaves and

2

chequered the rich-coloured moss beneath them.
Very ancient they were—nearly a thousand years,
it was thought, they had stood there and borne the
winter's snows and enjoyed the summer sunshine.
Wonderful messages all these years had they conveyed to the understanding eye and ear from their
great Creator; messages of faith and love, and, more
than all, of resurrection life. Hoary they were
now : moss and lichens covered their trunks, which
were of immense girth, and ferns waved their grace-
ful fronds from branch and trunk alike, clothing
the half-bare gnarled boughs with their wondrous
beauty.

Strange tales these oaks could have told of scenes
enacted in that castle—scenes of bloodshed and re-
venge, of suffering and sorrow. And no doubt
they could whisper of softer scenes also,—of love
and hope and joy. No wonder little Gretchen could
lie under their shade for hours and weave stories
which she fancied they whispered to her; whilst
she in return told them all her childish sorrows
and hopes, and believed that they sympathized in
them all, as none save Max did in her loveless
home. Poor little Gretchen! if only she had
known of One whose ear is never shut to the cry
of those for whom he gave his life; whose heart of
love yearns over the little children ; and whose

voice, though as yet unheard by her, was gently
whispering, "Come unto Me, and I will give you
rest."   Maybe one day, through the green leaves
of the old oaks, a child's voice would yet be
heard rising to heaven in songs of praise, " Hosanna
to the Son of God ! hosanna in the highest ! "
But not yet was that hymn to rise from Gretchen's
lips ; for whilst trees and flowers and birds alike fulfilled the purpose for which they were created, the
inmates of Oakwood Castle were content to live
without God, without a Saviour.   And yet a cry
was rising from more than one heart there towards
an unknown and therefore dreaded God.   And all
the while the oaks stood there preaching their
grand sermon ; and soul-stirring truths they did
preach of creating and upholding power and good-
ness—but they delivered no message of a living,
loving God-man Saviour : that message was to be
given by one who herself had heard the " Go in
peace, thy sins are forgiven thee ! " whispered in her
own heart.

Edith Trevor, now the wife of the young officer
Jack Ogilvie, the younger and only brother of the
Laird of Oakwood, was the orphan child of an old
English family, the Trevors of Trevor Hall.
Brought up by a fond uncle and aunt, her whole
life up to the time of her marriage had been one of

peace and love. Gentle words and loving caresses
had fallen to her portion, and coldness and want of
affection in family life was an experience of which
she knew nothing. Her husband, who was of a
much more loving and demonstrative nature than
the rest of the family, was deeply attached to his
young wife ; and knowing the sunny atmosphere of
love in which she had been brought up, dreaded
the effect the stately coldness and pride of his relations would produce on her. As yet he hardly
understood the young girl whom he had married.
Gentle (timid, he would have said), shrinking from
a harsh word or a hasty judgment passed on others,
there was yet a firmness of character and strength
of purpose shown when circumstances called them
forth that astonished him, and convinced him that,
despite his mother's stateliness and Hannah's abili-
ties, she would one day gain respect if not love from
both. Girl though she was, her mind was well
stored, and her knowledge of many subjects exten-
sive ; and through her lively winning manner there
was at times a depth of thought, and what he
termed seriousness, that perplexed him.

One book he saw was her daily study, and evi-
dently her great delight : that book was the Bible;
and he noticed, too, that from the reading of it she
rose bright and happy, with a peace shining in her

dark eyes that even he fancied had its source in a
love not of this world.

Yes, Edith Ogilvie had indeed the peace of God
ruling her heart and life, and the Word of God was
to her the joy and rejoicing of her heart.   Early
instructed in holy things, brought up to reverence
the name of Jesus, and to strive to keep his com-
mandments, yet the great change in her heart had
not really taken place at the time of her marriage ;
if it had we doubt if she would have united herself
to one who was a stranger to God.   It was when in
London on their marriage trip that the change took
place.   A heavy shower of rain had compelled her
and her husband to take shelter in a church nearer
at hand than the one they had intended going to.
It was a small building, more plain and unadorned
in its interior than any Edith had yet seen ; and
the service, which was in the Presbyterian form,
was unlike the one she was accustomed to.   The
preacher was a middle-aged man, who spoke with
a strong northern accent, not particularly eloquent ;
but the words were with power.   He spoke of
that he knew, "as a dying man to dying men," and
Edith listened with great interest.   His text was
the words of the eighteenth verse of the third chapter of First Peter : "Christ also hath once suffered
for sins. the just for the unjust, that he might bring

us to God." It was the simple declaration of the
glorious doctrine of substitution ; and as the young
wife listened the Holy Spirit blessed the preaching,
and she saw, as she had never seen before, the
greatness of the work that Jesus had done, not only
for all who believe, but for *her*. Like Christian
in the "Pilgrim's Progress," she left that church
singing in her heart,—

> "Blest cross, blest sepulchre, blest rather be
> The Man who there was put to death for me."

And that night she could say, as she never before
had said, "He loved *me*, and gave himself for me."

And from that day the love of Christ became
her constraining motive in all she did, and shed the
holy peace into her daily life which the quick eye
of her husband soon detected, though as yet he
only partly guessed the cause.

Four months had passed from that time ere the
day which found them on their way to Oakwood
Castle. Travelling as they did by stage-coach,
they saw more of the beauties of the country
through which they drove than we do now in the
days of railway travelling, and Edith's first peep of
Scottish scenery was a most favourable one. The
brightness and beauty of summer rested on the
hills and sparkled on the gently flowing rivers. The
larch "had hung all its tassels forth ; " and from

the woods and thickets the melody of sweet-singing
birds resounded. The country around Oakwood
was a pastoral one, and the sides of the grassy hills
were dotted over with sheep and little frisking
lambs.

The lumbering old carriage from the castle met
the young pair at the little town where the stage-
coach stopped, and after a kindly welcome from
the coachman, and the old butler who accompanied
him, the couple drove slowly to the castle, about
seven miles distant. It was evening ere they
reached it—a sweet summer evening. A mild gleam
was shed over all nature; the crows overhead
cawed as they hastened home to a large rookery
not far distant from Oakwood; and the sun was
just dipping behind the more distant ranges of
hills, his beams still falling on all around, and ting-
ing the light floating clouds with brilliant hues.
Ere the carriage stopped at the castle,—as they
drove down the long beautifully wooded approach,
Captain Ogilvie drew his wife's attention to the
fine old oaks, which, in the almost twilight of the
woods, looked dark and gloomy, yet seemed in their
own way to be giving a solemn, dignified welcome,
to the new-comers.

"Aren't they grand old trees, Edith?" he said.
"Why, I can almost fancy, like little Gretchen,

they are bidding us welcome to the ancestral home. In all Scotland there are no such oaks as these."

"They are, indeed, very fine trees, Jack, and make one think of the old times and superstitions of Druidical days. I shall never weary of looking at them. I am so glad to see the home of your childhood; it is a grand old place, and by God's blessing we shall have some happy days 'under the old oaks.'"

At the hall door, according to the old custom, the owner of the castle stood ready to bid them welcome, then led the way to the state-room, where his mother and sister sat. The old lady looked her best that evening, dressed, as was her wont on all great occasions, in a rich black satin robe, her gray hair simply braided beneath her widow's cap. Very grand and stately she looked as she rose to greet the couple; and though the kiss she pressed on her young daughter-in-law's brow seemed to her to be a frigid one, yet there was a light in the old lady's eye far softer than was usually there, as she turned towards her son; for if Mrs. Ogilvie had a tender feeling in her heart, it was the love she bore to him, her youngest child and his father's name-sake.

Very stiff was Hannah's manner towards her

stranger sister. One glance at her as she stood
timidly beside her husband, and Hannah, in her
usual abrupt way, passed judgment on her in her
mind as a silly, frightened young creature.

A few minutes' forced conversation, then a dead
silence reigned, broken by the lady of the house
asking Edith if she would like to change her dress,
as supper was waiting.

Very glad was Edith to escape even for a few
minutes from the stateliness and coldness of her
new relations.   Her heart was full,—her reception
had been so different from what she had expected :
her husband had not prepared her for this.   How,
she asked herself, would she get on with these
dreadfully stiff people, especially Hannah, who so
plainly showed she regarded her as a silly child ?
Her eyes filled with tears as she thought how often
she had pictured to herself the delight of having a
mother in Jack's parent, and a loving sister in
Hannah.   She was very young, and, I must confess, was nearly taking refuge in what a gifted
poetess calls

"Weak woman's tears, for relief."

When she looked out of the window, there stood
the old oaks, living witnesses of the upholding
power of the great Creator ; they, in their hoary
age, seemed to teach her a lesson of trust.   Their

Maker was her own loving Father in Christ Jesus;
and surely he who took care of the trees and
flowers of his own creating, would be near to help
her; and to her lips rose the precious promise, "Lo,
I am with you alway."

One moment of silent prayer for guidance, and
Edith stood ready to take her husband's arm and
go down to supper.   He looked at her, anxious to
know what she had thought of her welcome.   He
saw a slight remaining trace of tears in her dark
eyes, but through them the quiet peace shining
that at times so often puzzled him.   She smiled in
her own bright way, as she caught his look and in
part read his thoughts.   "It will come all right,
Jack," she said.   "You must help me not to be a
frightened little goose in the presence of your relations.   I feel strong when I lean on your arm."

He stooped over her, and whispered some en-
dearing words.   But as he watched her womanly
dignity and gentle bearing all that evening, and
noticed the peace and rest in her eyes, even he was
forced to confess that she was leaning on an arm
far stronger than his, of whose power he knew
nothing.

"Where are the children?" asked Edith of her
brother-in-law.   "Shall we not see them to-night?
I caught sight of a very handsome boy as we came

downstairs. But he suddenly vanished. It must have been Max, surely."

Mr. Ogilvie answered gravely, "Very probably it was so; but no one thinks him handsome, unless, indeed, it be Gretchen. The children are seldom downstairs. Their beds and schoolrooms are all in the oldest part of the castle, out of the way of the rooms we occupy,—there they disturb no one. You would not really care to see them."

"Indeed, I am longing to do so," she replied. "Poor little Gretchen! I have been looking forward so to fondling and caressing the little sufferer. It must be such a trial for a child like her to have to lie always on a couch. When I think how I used to run about in my childhood, I can hardly imagine how she bears it. You will let me love her, brother dear?" she said.

The father turned to her with a softer look on his countenance than it had worn for many a day. "Indeed," he said (but he lowered his voice as he spoke), "I shall be most grateful to you if you care at all for little Gretchen. My mother and sister don't like children, and are somewhat severe in discipline. And I do not see my way to interfere. They are thoroughly obedient, and seem to me not bad children, though Max is peculiar."

The remarks made on the young wife after she had retired to rest were as follows :—

"Jack certainly has chosen a beautiful wife," said Mrs. Ogilvie; "her features are perfect, and her whole bearing lady-like."

"Do you think so?" remarked Hannah. "Her eyes are good, I admit, but there is no character in her face. It is plain to see she has no decided opinions of her own—probably her mind is untrained, poor child; for Jack's sake, we must try to instruct her a little. She does not look, I grant, as if she would resent having her ignorance discovered. She has, I am sure, the thing of all others I despise, a meek spirit."

"What I have seen of her I like," interrupted the Laird of Oakwood; "and I cannot agree with Hannah regarding her want of character or knowledge. As to her meekness, is it not written somewhere in the Bible, that in the sight of God a meek and quiet spirit is of great price"?

To that speech there was no reply. God's standard of right and wrong was so entirely overlooked in that house, that any reference to it was met with surprise, if not dislike. Mrs. Ogilvie rose, and said it was more than time every one had gone to bed.

All unaware of the conversation regarding her,

Edith Ogilvie fell gently asleep, the words of the last blessed promise of the Saviour on her heart; and she dreamed that she heard them whispered in her ear by the summer wind as it rustled among the boughs as she lay "under the old oaks."

CHAPTER III.

THE MOTHERLESS CHILDREN.

"One cheering lesson seems impressed
    And taught by every word,—
How hearts whose echoes silent long
    No words of terror move,
May answer from their inmost depths
    To the soft call of love."

 GRETCHEN, she is as beautiful as an angel!" The speaker was Max Ogilvie, as he rushed into his sister's room on the evening of his uncle and aunt's arrival at the castle.

Gretchen raised herself in her bed, whither she was already ensconced for the night. "You have seen her then, Max? Do come and tell me all about her. Did she speak to you? and is she really as young as Aunt Hannah said?"

"Yes; I saw her, but not to speak to. She was just passing down the stair to go to supper, leaning on Uncle Jack's arm, and she looks very young— just like a girl; and she has dark, almost black, hair; and such lovely eyes, dark too, I am sure; and her lips were just like cherries: and, there now," said the boy, somewhat impatiently, " I can't describe her; but she's just like an angel, and you'll judge if I'm wrong. O Gretchen, if only I might play on the organ, I could tell you all about her; but Mr. Ross was not pleased with my Greek exercise to-day, and so he has forbidden me to touch it for a whole week. It is a great shame, for that punishes you as well as me."

" Never mind about me, Max: but I don't quite understand about Aunt Edith being dark, and yet like an angel; for angels, you know, have always golden hair and blue eyes."

" Have they?" said Max, dreamily.

" Yes, Max, *always;* at least in pictures."

" Come now, Master Max, it's full time you were away to your own bed, and had left Miss Gretchen in peace: say good-night, and go." And as she spoke, Agnes Craig, the old nurse, took the boy by the arm to expedite his retreat. Agnes kept as strong a hand over both children as any one in the house, and yet in her own way she loved them and humoured them more than any one else did, except the old butler Thomas.

So now ere he departed Max said coaxingly,

"I'm going this moment, Agnes; but first tell me what you think of this new aunt?"

"She's as pretty a lady as I ever saw, unless it be your ain mither, bairns. She was even prettier, wi' her golden brown hair and blue eyes. But there now; I'll no let anither word be spoken in this room the nicht; be off wi' ye."

The next morning at breakfast Edith was introduced to her young nephew. The introduction was such a formal one that, girl as she was, she had great difficulty in suppressing a laugh. "Mrs. Jack Ogilvie, this is my eldest and only grandson," said the stately old lady, leading Max forward by the hand, as if he had been a little child. "Make your bow and take your seat at the side-table, Max," she said. The boy flushed crimson, but bowed low to his girl-aunt; who, to the surprise of all in the room, drew him to her, and putting back his wavy brown hair, kissed his fair forehead, saying, "You and I will be great friends, Max, I hope. You must show me all your pets, and take me to your favourite haunts; and above all things, let me make the acquaintance of your little sister."

Max was as much astonished at this free and easy salutation as any one of the party, and answered in an embarrassed tone. He sat down subdued and silent, as usual, but with a great joy

"THIS IS MY ELDEST AND ONLY GRANDSON," SAID THE
STATELY OLD LADY.   (Page 32).

To face page 32

in his heart. That soft kiss seemed stamped on his
forehead : no one had ever kissed him since his
mother died, not even Gretchen,—she had been
forbidden to do so,—and even now he feared to
look up, in case he should see a frown of displea-
sure on Aunt Hannah's brow ; but that kiss and
those gentle loving words made Max his aunt's
devoted servant. More than once during breakfast Edith's eyes rested on the boy. Was it possible no one had perceived the beauty of that face,
with its finely moulded features, large gray eyes
with the fire of genius lighting them up, the high
forehead slightly concealed by the wavy golden-
brown locks that had a habit of falling over it ?
The countenance was a pensive one, and at times
she noted a far-off dreamy look pass over it, as if
the boy's thoughts were rambling in some far-dis-
tant region.

Once the father's eye glanced from Edith's to
his boy, and he read her admiration, and looked
more earnestly than he had ever done before at his
son. Yes, he confessed he was handsome that
day,—surely he had never looked like that before :
a flush was on his cheek, and the usual grave,
reserved air, he always wore in the presence of his
elders, had disappeared ; he held his head erect,
and an almost joyous sparkle was in his eyes. And

3

though the father knew it not, a few words spoken in love had wrought the change. Loving words, oh, why are they not oftener spoken!

The forenoon passed away somewhat heavily. The gentlemen had gone out on business to a neighbouring farm, and Edith, after having undergone a series of questions from her sister-in-law, all intended to expose her ignorance (which, however, she had answered with so much composure and evident acquaintance with the subjects spoken on, that even Hannah began to think she might probably be wrong as to the mental qualifications of the young wife), asked if she might take a stroll round the castle. Certainly, said Mrs. Ogilvie; but was it wise to go out so early, and whilst the sun shone so brightly? For her part, she never ventured out till later in the day; but perhaps Hannah would accompany her. And ere Edith could say she would on no account disturb either of them, but just saunter about till her husband's return, Hannah said in most decided terms, *She,* for one, had no idea of wasting time out of doors so early. She thought the morning hours should be devoted to mental improvement; she had a mathematical problem to solve, which would keep her fully occupied for some time; but if Mrs. Jack desired company, Nurse Craig would willingly

accompany her.   But Edith shook her head play-
fully, and ran off, declaring she was quite fit to
take care of herself.

In a few minutes she was out of doors, breathing
with perfect delight the sweet summer air, and
admiring the outer view of the grand old castle.
"Company, indeed!" she said to herself; "as if one
could ever feel alone in the midst of God's works of
nature."   Birds, trees and hills, and the sparkling
river, seemed all alike making holiday and rejoicing.
Instinctively she turned her steps to the old oaks,
thinking, as she gazed on them,—

> " What tales, if there were tongues in trees,
>   These giant oaks could tell
>   Of beings born and buried here;
>   Tales of the peasant and the peer;
>   Tales of the bridal and the bier—
>   The welcome and farewell."

As she neared them she heard a child's voice
low and soft, and the words, spoken apparently to
some one near, caught her ear : " All these hours
in the castle, and she's never come to see me ! and
I did so hope she would !   And 'cause she's so
young I thought maybe she would love me just a
wee bit, you know, though Aunt Hannah said she
would not, for nobody loves me : but she's wrong
there—Max *does*; and papa kissed me one day,
when I was very cross too ; and you dear old oaks,

you *do* love me, don't you ?   Oh dear ! oh dear ! I
do wish my own mamma had lived ; she loved me,
nurse told me so."

In a moment Edith was beside the speaker, and
started at finding there was no one near the little
girl, who lay on a couch placed under the shade of
the old oaks.

"Dear little Gretchen," she said, " I am so glad
to see you ; but indeed it is not my fault I have
not done so long ere this. Your papa said I could
not see you last night, and this morning grandmamma thought it was time enough by-and-by.
But now, darling, you and I must be great com-
panions."   And she folded the little half-terrified
child in her arms, her eyes filling with tears as she
noticed the dark lines which suffering had drawn
under the large blue eyes.

For a minute the child was too surprised for
speech. Was she dreaming ? or was this some
woodland nymph who dwelt, as Gretchen had so
often fancied, in the old oaks, and who had heard
her lamentations and come to comfort her ?   But
Edith's question, "Can you love me, little Gretchen, do you think, and let me fill the place of
mother to you ?" broke the spell, and the child
burst into tears.

"Oh, do, do love me, Aunt Edith," she sobbed ;

"only Max does, and— ;" then she paused. Some day, she thought, she would tell this beautiful aunt all about her friends the old oaks, but not now.

Edith noticed the pause, and interpreted it thus : " And Jesus ; is that it, darling ? "

" Jesus ! oh no. Do you mean the Son of God ? Oh, he does not love me. I'm not good at all ; and besides," she said, as if speaking to herself, " I know so little about him, and he's so far off."

" Far off, my darling ! He is not so. Do you know, Gretchen, he is so near, he is even now listening to all our words, and longing to hear you ask him to bless you and make you his own little child ? "

She was hardly prepared for the look of wondering surprise and doubt that came into the little girl's eyes as she said, " Who ? Jesus ! I don't understand what you mean. How could I speak to him ? "

Just at that moment the sound of footsteps was heard, and looking up Edith met the eyes of her brother-in-law fixed with wonder, and yet with evident pleasure, on the scene before him. Was it possible, he was asking himself, that his little suffering girl would really find a friend and comforter in her beautiful young aunt ? But he spoke

not to the child, only addressed Edith, telling her
his brother had gone in-doors to seek her.

"Ah, well," she said, "he will find me here.
Gretchen and I are just making the acquaintance
of each other, and are not yet willing to part company;—are we, dear?"

One glance from the child-eyes answered the
question; a glance so full of softness, love, and
gratitude, that the father involuntarily turned away
with a quick pang in his heart, as that look told
him how his suffering child had been longing for
affection denied her. Had he been right, he questioned, in withholding the fatherly caresses he had
often longed to bestow? Was it possible his little
Gretchen had been yearning all the time for a
parent's love? If he had any doubts on the subject, they were speedily removed, for just then his
brother came to claim his wife, and he stood alone
with Gretchen under the old oaks.

"Where is nurse?" he said. "Are you alone,
Gretchen?"

A contented little voice answered, "Oh, she will
be here by-and-by. I like being alone." Then
lowering her voice, she said, "Kiss me, papa, just
once, like what you did *one* day."

The request from her lips was a strange one, and
her very voice seemed changed. He stooped, and,

for almost the first time since her mother's death, took her in his arms and kissed her, not once but many times.

"What makes you look like that, Gretchen?" he inquired.

"'Cause I'm so happy. O papa, could you love me a bit, just a wee bit? Aunt Edith says she will; Max will be so glad."

The father answered with another kiss, then strode with rapid steps away, and sought the solitude of his own room. Here he remained some time lost in thought, a picture of a young girl, with eyes like Gretchen's, and fair sunny hair, before him. With bitter anguish the proud reserved man was telling himself—ay, and his too often forgotten God—that he had failed, bitterly failed, in his duty to his motherless children. He saw now that even one little gleam of love, such as he had denied her, had brought joy to the eyes of little wayward Gretchen, such as he had never seen there since she was a very young child. But, he was asking himself bitterly, how could he get his mother and sister to believe that love and kindness were as necessary a part of a child's training as cold reserve and comparative harshness? Perhaps his sister-in-law would come to his help in the matter, and by the influence of her loving heart and meek and quiet spirit, aid him in carrying out the change of training.

The next day he resolved he would visit the children in their play-room, and try to interest himself in their pleasures and pursuits. Truly "man proposes, but God disposes," for ere he could carry out his intentions, the quiet household at Oakwood Castle were in sore perplexity and trouble, in the midst of which all thoughts of a change of plan as regarded the children's up-bringing were postponed, if not forgotten.

But in the meantime little Gretchen was lying in peace and happiness, pondering over some of her young aunt's words, and fancying that the old oaks were entering into her joy, as she gently whispered, whilst the summer wind sighed through their branches, "She said she loved me, she loved me; and papa kissed me, he kissed me; and I'm glad, so glad." And all the while the little sunbeams glinted down through the green foliage, and played on the fair hair of the child, and danced on the little white hands, and seemed to rejoice in her gladness, just as if they had known all about it, and were rejoicing that the little lonely child had got a friend.

Max found her in the evening, when his studies were over, with a look of peace and joy on her face

such as he had never witnessed there; and the
two children, as they sat together, spoke of their
beautiful young aunt as some bright angel who
had suddenly come into their midst, and by her
sweet looks and loving words brought light and
sunshine into their lives. Wistful looks Max cast
that evening at his beloved organ. There were so
many emotions at work in his heart which he had
no words to express, which nevertheless he could
tell forth in music. But he could sing; and
scarcely knowing why, he chose a psalm of praise,
and Gretchen's sweet voice chimed in as together
they sang, to a grand old tune, words learned as a
task not long before—

> " Give praise and thanks unto the Lord,
>   For bountiful is he;
>   His tender mercy doth endure
>   Unto eternity."

I hardly know whether or not they really recog-
nized the joy that had fallen into their lives as
being sent by God, so entirely had they been
brought up in ignorance of him as a personal God
who careth for his creatures. But when the psalm
had ceased, Gretchen said, half to herself, "I
wonder if Jesus heard? *She* says he's always
near."

Max looked up at her as if asking an explana-

tion, when the door opened, and their grandmother
came in to pay her usual formal evening visit.

"Now, children," she said, "it is quite time for
you both to be in bed. I disapprove of these late
talks; Gretchen looks feverish as it is. Max, you
should have more sense than to allow her to excite
herself. And where is nurse? Ah! here she
comes now. Good-night, Gretchen, and do try
to give as little trouble getting undressed as possible.—And by the way, Max, I have to tell you
that, as a very great treat, you are to be allowed
to accompany our party to-morrow to see the
waterfall distant some twelve miles. It appears to
me a most irregular proceeding, to think of taking
a boy from his studies to see any sight; but your
Uncle Jack asked as a favour that you might go,
and your father agreed at once : so let me see that
you behave yourself, and keep as much in the
background as possible. Of course, Mr. Ross will
attend to you. Good-night;" and with a cold
shake of the hand the old lady withdrew, quite
satisfied that she had fulfilled her duty in thus
paying her usual nightly visit to the children.

Had she found them naughty, she would have
punished them; or ill, she would have prescribed
the necessary remedies; and by doing these things
she thought she performed her duty towards

them even as she had done to her own children. That love should form a part of their training was an idea that had never occurred to her, chiefly because she was herself ignorant of the "God of love," who sends bright gleams of his wondrous love into every human life if only they will look to him in Christ Jesus and receive it.

Ere long Max and Gretchen fell asleep with a sweeter sense of peace and happiness in their young hearts than they had ever previously felt, produced by the powerful influence of a few Christ-like loving words.

CHAPTER IV.

THE WATERFALL.

"The fall of waters and the song of birds,
And hills that echo to the distant herds,
Are luxuries excelling all the glare
The world can boast and her chief favourites share."

THE next day proved a lovely one, the gray morning giving place to all the glories of July sunshine and a bright blue sky, with small fleecy cloudlets forming all sorts of fantastic figures thereon. Never had Max felt so happy as, when seated outside the old family coach, he was driving through a country unfamiliar to him, although he had spent some years of his young life in the immediate neighbourhood of it. Very varied was the scenery through which they passed : now through woods, with their "leafy tide of greenery still rippling up the wind;" then, for miles, amid the solitude of the hills, where scarce a human form was seen, and even a cottage was a rarity,—sheep, sheep on all sides, were alone visible, climbing the steep slopes of the grassy hills. Every spot on the road had some wild tradition of bygone days allotted to it; every one of the solitary dells had in olden time been peopled in the imaginations of the inhabitants by legions of spiritual creatures; and even the boy half fancied he discerned on the hill-tops and in the lonely glens a brownie peeping out, as if taking a view of the advancing party.

"How grand those hills are!" said Edith; "though the solitude here seems almost overpowering. Surely the inhabitants of the few scattered cottages we have passed must lead very lonely lives!"

"So one would think," said her brother-in-law; "but they do not appear to find it so. Custom does much; and busied in their own simple affairs, with plenty to occupy them, they never feel lonely, they say. But stop a little, and you shall judge for yourself. We will rest the horses by-and-by at a cottage in one of the most lonely spots amongst the hills. My brother's bride will be welcomed there, and you will receive a true answer as to their loneliness from the inmates. But look! there is a distant peep of the upper part of the waterfall we have come to see; presently we will retrace our steps and climb that steep path to the left, and so

see the fall in all its beauty. The loch from which
the fall issues is about a mile above it, but to-day
we cannot visit it."

Edith's admiration of the wild scenery pleased
Mrs. Ogilvie, and even Hannah, who interspersed
a remark now and then as to the great superiority
of Scottish over all scenery in the world, hardly
appearing to notice the satirical remark of her
soldier-brother : "You must be a great authority
on that subject, Hannah, considering you have
never been out of Scotland in your life."

At last the cottage inn, for such it was, was
reached,—a very humble little abode. Here the
party alighted, and after partaking of the simple
fare to be obtained there, consisting of bannocks
and butter, cheese and milk, they were to walk to
the fall. An old woman, in a clean short-gown
and snowy mutch, with a black handkerchief tied
down it (the sign of widowhood), welcomed them
warmly, asking the laird kindly about his "mither-
less bairns," and patting the young English bride
on her shoulder, praying the Lord to bless her.
Max, too, was made much of, and addressed by a
term new to him,—the "young laird;" "and a
right weel-faured ane too," she whispered to his
father; "though we mauna forget the Lord looketh
at the heart, no at the outward man.—Hae ye

ta'en the Lord as the guide o' your youth, young maister?" she said. But at that question his grandmother called Max to her side, and it remained unanswered.

"These sort of people are so forward," Hannah afterwards remarked. "Such a question to put to a child!"

"And yet," Edith replied, "it was a very natural one, and I am sure she meant it kindly."

Left alone a few minutes with the old woman and her married daughter, who also lived in the cottage, Edith asked if they were not dull in this solitary spot.

"Nae, nae, my dear young leddy, we're no that dull—there's nae time for that. 'Tis true we're mair nor ten miles awa frae the town, and sax miles frae the nearest kirk, sae the bairns are auld ere they can win to the Lord's hoose,—but the aulder anes o' us walk ilka Sabbath across the hills even in the winter to hae that privilege, and whiles the minister comes to see us; but ye see we canna weel feel lanesome, though we are nigh on to four miles frae ony neighbour, for we're a guid big family oursels, and our folks hae lived in this cottage for generations. Ye see, ma'am, it maun be a shepherd lives here, to tend the sheep on the hills, and my faither was ane, sae I was born here;

and when the Lord took him to himself, my husband (wha was a shepherd likewise) got his place, and he bided on here; and when he in his turn was ta'en, my dochter's husband, wha was the under-shepherd, got the place, sae they would just hae me live on wi' them, and I can help them, for they hae a wheen bairns. Then, ye see, we hae a bit o' land o' our ain, so there's aye plenty to do—and the day we are hay-making; and then wi' the cow to look after, and cheese and butter to make, there's nae time for idleness. And we're content wi' the place the Lord has allotted to us, and them that's *that* can ne'er be ill off. And we hae the collies for company, specially in the winter, when there's nae grass on the hills to be gotten, for the snaw lies deep here, and so we hae to send the sheep, puir beasties, awa' down to a field town-wise, wherein they can feed wi' neeps and sic like, so the dogs bide wi' us; and gude company they are, leddy, sae wise, and cannie too. And in the summer days we whiles hae company like yoursel' look in on us to see the fall, sae we hae nae reason to speak about dulness. Besides, we hae aye the company o' the Lord himself, and that makes a place bonnie. You's nae tak offence at an auld woman askin' you, young mistress, gif you love our Lord Jesus Christ?"

"Offence—oh no," said Edith; "I love to hear any one speak of him, though it is only lately I have learned to love him; but now I could not live without him. I wonder no longer that you do not feel lonely, if he is your friend.—Is the shepherd calling one much liked?"

"Ay, ay, 'tis weel eneuch liked, my leddy; but oh, amang the hills here it's dangerous, rale dangerous: my gudeman and my auldest son baith lost their lives on the hills tendin' the sheep. Ye see, there are awfu' deep scaurs in the hills, and ae winter day, afore the snaw was deep, but when the rocks were slippery wi' ice, my gudeman saw a sheep had climbed up a rale steep rocky bit, and was biddin' fair to be lost, and he gaes after it, and lost his footing, and fell down the steep scaur. He was found and brocht hame to me, still livin' and conscious, but afore we could get a doctor he had breathed his last in my arms, just saying the words of the psalm he likit sae weel to sing,—

> 'Yea, though I walk in death's dark vale,
>   Yet will I fear none ill:
> For thou art with me; and thy rod
>   And staff me comfort still.'

And no twa years after that, my bonnie stalwart laddie, nineteen years o' age, met wi' the like fate; only it was waur for his puir mither, for he fell

into the water frae a height and was drowned,
sae I had nae partin' words frae him to comfort
me : but I doubt nae he too is wi' the Lord, for at
the time o' his faither's death he received the
effectual call, and ever after he walked as became
a child o' God.   The Lord gave, and the Lord hath
ta'en away ; blessed be the name o' the Lord."

Edith's eyes were filled with tears as she listened
to the sad tale, told so simply, yet so pathetically ;
she spoke some words of comfort, alluding to the
Good Shepherd who gave his life for us.   As
she raised her head she saw Max standing beside
them, waiting silently till their conversation was
ended to deliver his message, to the intent that
the party were awaiting his aunt to join them and
proceed to the fall.   Edith shook hands kindly
with the old woman, who gave her a parting
blessing, saying, "The Lord be with you in all
times of trouble ; and dinna forget this : 'Through
much tribulation we maun enter into the king
dom.' "

Edith could hardly account for the sense of fore-
boding that these words left on her spirit ; and a
sudden question arose in her mind as to whether
she could trust and love the Lord if trouble fell
on her, as fully as she could now when life was
full of brightness ?   Oh, she had yet to learn the

full faithfulness of her Father in heaven, and to experience the truth of his promise, that his children shall have strength granted to them according to their day.

The waterfall was reached at last, and the whole party stood gazing with admiration at the feathery foam as it dashed down from a height of nearly three hundred feet. Max stood a little apart, drinking in with all the force of his enthusiastic nature the glories of the scene, his ear catching and retaining the new and wondrous sounds produced by the fall of the cataract and the thunder of the stream below. So engrossed was he that he forgot the presence of the whole party, and, in a tone of almost impatience, gave utterance to the wish of his heart,—"Oh, if only Mr. Ross would let me play the organ to-night, I could almost make Gretchen see all this; I am sure I could, if I tried at once."

He started as a voice said, "Max, what do you mean?" and looking round, saw his father looking at him with a countenance full of perplexity. "How," he went on, "could you make Gretchen see this fall by playing on the organ?"

The boy flushed crimson. "O papa," he said, "I can't explain it rightly; if only I might try, I know I could. Gretchen understands the organ,

and it seems to bring before her just the things I
want it to do; but Mr. Ross has forbidden me to
play on it for some days yet, and ere then the
sounds may have gone from me. O father, if I
might only play just to-night!"

"No, Max, I cannot ask Mr. Ross to lessen a
punishment which you fully deserve for carelessly
prepared exercises," were the words rising to his
father's lips, when something checked them. For
once he thought he would try the power of kindness, rather than punishment. The pleading look
in his boy's eyes touched his heart; so he said
pleasantly, "Well, Max, I'll speak to Mr. Ross
about it."

Just then the tutor approached them, and Mr.
Ogilvie told him the boy's request; adding, that if
Mr. Ross would shorten the sentence of punishment,
he would be pleased. Mr. Ross at once did so,
saying that Master Max had already made up for
his carelessness by extra diligence.

The boy's face beamed with joy, as he stood
more rapt than ever in delight with all the scene
around him. Mr. Ross eyed him for a moment
with wonder; then turned away, saying, with a
sigh of perplexity, to Mr. Ogilvie: "Master Max
is no common boy, sir; every day I see it more.
There is something in him that I understand not;

nay, that I think none of us understand aright.
I am no musician, as you know, sir; but when
that boy plays the organ, my whole soul is moved.
It is as if it became like a living creature, and
poured forth every emotion of the lad's nature.
You could almost declare it speaks. He is a good
scholar on the whole, but I believe in music he is
a rare genius. And of late I have been thinking
whether, sir, we are right in not encouraging him
in that matter. Some day, I believe, he will make
a name in the musical world."

The father started at these words, said by such
a reflective man as his old preceptor; and once
again a pang of shame filled his heart, to think he
hardly knew his boy was musical. He could not
recall having heard him play. Sometimes he had
heard the organ sounding through the house, and
heard his sister Hannah remark, "There is Max
wasting his time, as usual, drumming on the organ."
But whenever he opened the play-room, the music
had invariably stopped, and he had thought no
more about it.

But that night, when the distant tones of the
organ pealed through the castle, Mr. Ogilvie
quietly left the guest-chamber, and stole to the
play-room door. He listened long; as one entranced he stood. Scene after scene through

which they had that day passed rose before his eyes as the boy played. Now it was the ripple of the wind amid the leafy branches of the woods, then the dark sparkling river; anon the solemn silence of the hills, broken only by the plaintive bleating of the sheep; again the wondrous dash of the mountain cataract, as it whirled and foamed into the stream below. The whole scene was truly produced, concluding with a wonderful anthem of praise to the God of creation. One day the boy would cause his loved organ to produce a higher anthem,—

> " In truest unison with choir above,
> For prelude to a loftier, sweeter strain—
> The praise of God's inestimable love,
> Who sent redemption to a world of woe,
> That all a Father's heart his banished ones might know."

But to that love he was as yet a stranger. In the depth of his own heart he must experience the power of the love of Christ, ere he could tell it forth, and praise aright the King of kings.

The father waited till the last chord had swelled on the air, and gently died out, then turned away; his heart was full. He had made a great discovery. Mr. Ross was right — his boy was a genius. His emotion was so great he could not yet return into the guest-chamber; so he went out in the gray twilight, and paced up and down "under the shadow of the old oaks." The silvery moonbeams stole through the leaves as the evening breeze shook them gently, and fell on the green moss beneath, and touched the old gnarled trunks with a new beauty. The calm loneliness of the scene soothed his spirit, and remembering the fancies of little Gretchen, he could almost have imagined that the oaks understood and partici pated in his emotion. But he longed for human sympathy; and re-entering the house, the cold, reserved man, found himself almost unconsciously pouring out the whole story to his sister-in-law— so attractive is the influence of one who is a true follower of the loving Jesus, of a heart "at leisure from itself" to soothe and sympathize.

CHAPTER V

> " Wait till the trial is over,
> And take thy heart again ;
> For as gold is tried by fire,
> So a heart must be tried by pain."

"SO the old minister at Queenshope has at last obtained a colleague," said the Laird of Oakwood, addressing his mother. The whole family were seated at the breakfast-table, some of them busily engaged opening letters and papers.

"Who says so?" replied, or rather queried, the old lady. "We have heard so long about this wonderful colleague, that I, for one, have ceased to expect he will ever come,—although it is certainly to be desired that the church at Queenshope should be re-opened. The one in the village is so far away, it is impossible children and delicate people can walk so far. It was a pity when old Mr. Walker had to give up preaching."

" Ah, well, mother, truth to say, 'twas time he did, for his sermons were strange productions, and fitted only to set one to sleep. It is said this Mr. Murray is a man of different stamp : he is to preach on Sunday, so we can go and hear him."

" Well," was the response, " I do hope he'll preach morality, and teach the young to honour and obey their parents, and servants to reverence their masters."

Mr. Ogilvie's face grew thoughtful. " Yes, mother," he said gravely, " these things are all right in their place ; but I fancy something more is needed, though I hardly know what."

Just then he looked across to his brother, who, engrossed in a large letter, had taken no part in the conversation, and one glance at his face suddenly turned his tide of thought. What could be the matter ? for the young officer had turned deadly pale, and was strangely agitated. He held the letter so as to screen his face from his wife, and making some excuse, left the room. Edith looked up amazed, but Hannah's declaration, " There was nothing wrong ; just like Jack to leave the room so abruptly," silenced her.

The meal over, the laird anxiously sought his brother. He found him out of doors, pacing up and down in great agitation, with an official letter in his hand. "Oh, George," he said, as his brother approached, "how shall I tell her, my darling Edith? Look here;" and he showed him the letter desiring him instantly to rejoin his regiment, which was then stationed in Ireland, as it, along with several others, had received orders to go, under the command of Sir Arthur Wellesley, to take part in the Peninsular War, and they were to sail as soon as possible.

In a moment Mr. Ogilvie saw all. Such an order entailed that the young wife must be left behind; and for how long none could tell. What comfort could he give? The shock would be great; they had had no thoughts of this. At last he faltered out the words, "She is a soldier's wife, Jack, and will act like one. God help her!"

"And He will," said the husband. "She loves and serves Him, my gentle Edith. But where shall I leave her? Her uncle and aunt have already taken another niece, who is an orphan and homeless, to fill her place, and I know Edith would not for one moment think of turning her out."

His brother interrupted him. "Leave her here, Jack; this is the best place for her till the war is over. I will, trust me, act a true brother's part to her, and comfort her as best I can."

A warm pressure of his hand was the response

he got; but he saw still a shade of doubt rested on his brother's face. "But my mother and Hannah," he said—"they may not be willing; and even if they were, I question if Edith would be altogether at home with them, they are so unlike, and—"

"Never fear, Jack: I do believe that wife of yours will win every heart in this house yet, and be a blessing to us all in more ways than one. She has done me good already, and brought a light into my children's young lives that never shone there before. I believe we are entertaining 'an angel unawares.' Don't fear for Edith, Jack; suffer she will—how much, I tremble to think; but she has a something that will bear her up. I hardly know what it is, but I feel she has it."

"Yes," said her husband, and his strong manly voice trembled as he spoke; "she has a *Friend* who will never fail her;—would he were my friend too! But the news must be broken to her. I feel as if I could do so easier here. Send her to me, George, and do you prepare my mother."

The laird started off, his heart full of compassion for the young couple, with a parting before them which might be "unto death." Looking round, he saw his brother had sought the quiet shelter of the old oaks, and there he would send his wife.

Of that parting scene we will not write much; they that have gone through the like can figure it to themselves. The suddenness of the blow, the bitter pang of leaving him whom she loved so dearly, the thought of dwelling amongst strangers, and some of those so uncongenial, all overwhelmed the young wife, and for a while hindered her from raising her thoughts to the Friend who would never leave her. "Oh, take me with you, take me with you!" was the cry on her lips; and bitter indeed were the tears shed that day beneath the old oaks. It may be, in days gone by, they had been witnesses of like scenes, when knights, clad in panoply of war, had beneath their shade said farewell to loved ones; but never had they sheltered truer or more loving hearts than they did on that summer day. Long they sat, these two, thankful for the thick canopy of leaves which hid them from all eyes;—thankful too for the peace and quiet of Nature, which seemed to soothe their spirits. There was much to say, for that very night must see the young officer on his way to the post of duty.

Edith shrank keenly from the thought of remaining in the castle, but yielded when she saw that it was her husband's wish she should do so. "You can do good here, love," he whispered.

" Your loving spirit will win all hearts by-and-by; and maybe not to yourself alone, but— ; " here he paused. She looked eagerly up, and he said softly, " to the Friend *you* love, Edith."

Then, through her tears, she spoke to her husband of Jesus, and entreated him to make him his Friend also. And there, under the old oaks, husband and wife knelt together, and poured out their hearts to Him who hears and answers prayer; and the bitterness of the parting was softened to Edith by the sweet hope that her loved husband had begun to lean on that arm whose strength she was daily finding almighty to help.

Throughout the whole castle there was grief when the news spread of Jack's departure. The old lady, though she gave way to no outward emotion, grieved at heart ; and when she gave her son a parting kiss, it was with deep emotion she promised to take care of his young wife till his return : and even Hannah was moved a little out of her frigid manner. Captain Ogilvie was himself not a little astonished when Max, whom he had always regarded as a child, stepped boldly forward, saying, " Uncle, I will do everything I can to comfort and help Aunt Edith, I love her so much ; and Gretchen will too : won't you give us a little bit of charge of her as well as grand-

mamma and Aunt Hannah?" His uncle pressed
his hand, saying, "God bless you, Max. Yes,
truly I believe you and Gretchen can do much to
comfort your poor aunt. I leave her to you also;
she will need all the comfort you can give her.
Farewell;" and he was off, his last kiss resting on
Edith's lips, his last word whispered in her ear,
"I leave you in God's keeping, my own darling;
pray for me."

His brother accompanied him to the little town
where he was to catch the stage-coach. Their
hearts were too full for speech, but in that very
silence these two understood each other better
than they had ever done before. One parting
word—"Take care of my darling: and, O George,
let her be left alone for some days; her heart is
too full for words yet."

"Trust me, I'll see to that," was the reply; and
the Laird of Oakwood only waited till he saw the
coach roll away, then slowly drove home in the
moonlight.

Edith heard the carriage-wheels, as she lay in
her bed striving in vain to stay her tears. One
thought would rise again and again to her heart,
"What if this parting be unto death?" Then
the words of the old woman in the shepherd's
cottage came to her remembrance, "'Tis through

much tribulation we must enter into the kingdom."
The wind had arisen and was making sweet melody
amongst the leaves outside, but somehow to her
ears it was more like a wail of sadness than a song
of joy. And when at dawn of day sleep closed
her weary eyes (only to make the waking more
bitter), in her ears the sough, sough of the wind in
the branches of the old oaks seemed to sound as a
refrain the words, "Through much tribulation we
must enter into the kingdom." But while she
slept, the loving eyes of her heavenly Father, who
slumbers not nor sleeps, were bent on his suffering
child, and a voice in her heart, stronger than the
wind amongst the oaks, was whispering, "Fear
not, for I am with thee. I will never leave thee
nor forsake thee."

CHAPTER VI.

THE YOUNG MUSICIAN.

" Oh ! surely melody from heaven was sent
    To cheer the soul when tired with human strife ;
To soothe the wayward heart by sorrow rent,
    And soften down the rugged road of life."

"FOUR whole days, Max, and Aunt Edith has never left her room ! I am so very, very sorry for her ;—only think, it may be years ere she sees Uncle Jack again. Nurse says so,—and she loves him. How I wish I could do anything to comfort her."

The speaker was little Gretchen, whose tender heart yearned over the gentle aunt from whose lips she had heard such loving words. If only, she thought, she could have got admittance to her aunt's room, who knows but she might have consoled her. Oh, if only she could see her once more, even for a minute. But all these days Edith remained shut up in her room, gentle and patient, but unable to rouse herself, or even to return thanks for kindness. One wish she expressed,—to be left alone; and Mr. Ogilvie, true to the promise made to his brother, contrived that it should be so.

But now it was evident to all that it was advisable she should exert herself. Hannah's expostulations, and the old lady's quieter remarks as to the duty of ceasing to mope, were alike useless; in fact, Edith hardly appeared to notice them in these first days of sorrow. It was almost as if faith, trust, and sense of duty had left her heart; she felt nothing but a dreadful void, and a weary, hopeless sense of despair.

Let us not judge her harshly; she was young, and the blow had come so suddenly. Can we not remember some such time in our own lives, when the very sunshine seemed hateful, and we doubted even the tender mercies of Him "whose nature and whose name is love"?

But not long would the Lord allow a true child of his to remain thus cast down. The still, quiet voice of the Holy Spirit began to speak to the sorrowing one, and to whisper that she had a work to do for the Lord she loved. That evening she rose and left her room; as she did so, the rich soft tones of the organ fell on her ear, and determined her first of all to visit the children in their room.

The door stood ajar, and as Max's back was to it, she stood for some moments unobserved, listening to the wonderful music the young musician was producing. She was not long in comprehending the nature of it ;—it was a wail of sorrow, mingled with tender sympathy and comfort. Wonderfully soothing it was. Not a word of sympathy would the strange boy have uttered in words, but seated at his loved organ, the real feelings of his heart found utterance. Truly of him it might have been said, in the words of the poet,—

> " He lived in that ideal world
> Whose language is not speech, but song."

It was Gretchen who first saw her aunt—who, signing to her to be silent, slipped quietly beside her, and seating herself near the couch, drew the child lovingly into her arms, and waited till Max ceased playing.

"Aunt Edith here!" he exclaimed when he saw her, and flushed crimson at the thought she had heard his music. She called him to her side, and thanked him for the sweet comfort and sympathy he had given her ; then with a full heart she spoke to the brother and sister of the Friend who was with her, and would enable her to bear up under all trials.

" Is it Jesus ? " asked Gretchen. " You said he knows all about us, and cares. Is it true ? "

" Yes, darling, quite true." And there and then the young wife spoke to these motherless children of Jesus, his life, his love, and his atoning death. They listened eagerly. The story of redeeming love was new to them, and God was only known as one to be feared—yea, rather dreaded.

" Does he really care for us, and wish us to love him ? " said Gretchen.

" Yes ; he is saying to-day, and to you, ' Give me your heart ; come unto me.' He can brighten the darkest lot, and comfort the saddest heart. Oh, what could I do without him now ? He so loved us as to die for us. He loves us still ; he has said, ' Lo, I am with you alway.' Won't you come to him, and let him save you ? "

It was Gretchen's child-voice that whispered, " I will.—O Jesus, save me ! "

A voice broke the silence. " Master Max, your Aunt Hannah wishes to speak to you."

All started at the voice, and turning her head, Edith saw Mr. Ross standing beside her. How long he had stood there she knew not. She greeted him kindly, and read his sympathy for her in the look of his eye. The old man had a kind heart, hid away beneath a stiff exterior, and he felt deeply for the wife of his old pupil, left thus alone in a strange house. He had overheard much of her conversation with the children, and felt at once the source from whence she drew comfort, and by-and-by would obtain strength to endure.

She rose now, saying she must go downstairs. On the way her brother-in-law met her, and leaning on his arm she entered the keeping-room, where she was kindly welcomed by Mrs. Ogilvie ; and even Hannah said, in a softer voice than usual, she was glad to see she had raised herself at last,— trouble of any kind was only increased by moping over it. For her part, since her brother's departure she had found comfort in increased study; concentrating the mind on some special subject being particularly useful. As she spoke, she looked at the sweet face of her sister-in-law ; and the look of calm trust and peace shining there through the sadness impressed her and somehow silenced her. She felt, though she would not confess it even to herself, that Edith had obtained a higher comfort than even intellectual pursuits could have given her.

The moon was shining softly, touching the hills around the old castle with a lurid light, ere Edith retired to rest that night ; but on her spirit a great calm had descended — a love deeper than any earthly one was filling her heart. In full confidence of faith she committed her beloved husband into the hands of her heavenly Father, and rejoiced she had yet on earth a work to do for Him who had redeemed her. She saw much opposition awaiting her; she might have to bear harsh words, and even reproaches; but, by God's grace, she knew that love would win the day, and in faith she prayed that the love of Christ which passeth understanding might take captive every heart in Oakwood Castle.

To show forth by life and lip that love, became the work of her life. Already that work had begun. Little Gretchen had fallen asleep with a new peace in her heart, the dawn of a new joy begun in her suffering life. There was One then, she said to herself, who cared for her, and longed for her love—One who, even if the only friend (save Max) from whose lips she had heard loving words, were removed far from her, would abide with her and love her for ever. She had grasped this knowledge with the simple, trustful faith of a little child; and verily such a faith hath its reward. She would have a new story now to tell the old oaks the next time she lay beneath their shade; and even in sleep the words they seemed to sing to her came very near to the ones which are now sung in

so many households, and are joined in by so many
childish voices, —

> " I am so glad that Jesus loves me;
> Jesus loves even me."

It was the old, old story, adapted to every age,
bringing joy to many hearts, peace and good-will
to men; "old, and yet ever new.

Many a raid had in the olden time been made on
the strong castle; again and again had it been
called on to surrender in vain; but that night
One sought admittance there, knocking at the
closed doors of many hearts, with " pierced hands
and crowned hair," who would, by the power of
love, prove more than conqueror.

CHAPTER VII

THE COTTAGE IN THE GLEN.

> " What lacks my heart, that makes it
>   So weary and full of pain
> That trembling Hope forsakes it,
>   Never to come again?
> Only the sound of a voice,
>   Tender, and sweet, and low,
> That made the earth rejoice
>   A year ago."

"OH, but my heart's wae for the puir bairn wife," said Nurse Craig, addressing the old butler, a few weeks after the captain's departure. "She gaes about sae sad-like, and yet sae patient and calm; and whiles ain would think she's fair bowed down wi' sorrow, then the next minute you'll see a smile on her face and a licht in her eye, as if she had some deep-down well o' comfort in her heart naething can dry up. I canna understand it. And what a power she has gotten ower Miss Gretchen! I can scarce believe she's the same

bairn, so gentle now, quieted in her most fretful
days by a word or a glance o' the young lady's
een, far mair than she ever was by her aunt's hard
words or the old lady's punishments."

"Aweel," said the coachman, James Duncan,
who had overheard the nurse's conversation, "for
my pairt, I misdoubt her; she hasna the queenly
look o' our ain ladies, nor their talents either, I'm
thinking I heard Miss Hannah say ain day. If
there were only some folks to teach bairns to obey
their parents, and no insist on taking their own
ways, it would be better for us a'; and I maun
say our ain Miss Hannah tries whiles to do that,
though maybe she's no a gude hand wi' the young.
For my pairt, I'd sooner manage a dozen pair o'
horses, than ain young lassie, sae wilfu' they are
noo-a-days. There's my Nanny, for a' the trouble
her mother and me have taken wi' her, naething
can satisfy her noo but she maun gang off to
Edinbro' to seek a place, and see some o' the
world, she says; and never a word o' reason will
she listen to, and the gudewife ailing, too. It's ill
tae ken what women would be at;" and so saying,
the coachman rose and went to look after his
horses.

His cottage stood at a little distance from the
castle, at the head of a lonely glen, whose wooded

banks sloped down to the bed of a dancing rivulet, which here and there dashed noisily over the large rocky stones which impeded its course. A lovely spot it was, so quiet and retired that one would have said the inmates of the neat-looking cottage, o'ercanopied with trees, must lead a peaceful life; but the face of a young girl, who stood at the cottage door on the summer day we are writing of, spoke of anything rather than peace. And yet the face was a good one, thoughtful and intelligent; but an expression of discontent, mingled with sorrow, marred its beauty. An older woman sat beside her at a spinning-wheel, which she had moved outside to enjoy the sunshine.

"Nanny," she was saying in a vexed tone, "whatever has come to ye? Never a turn's work have ye done to-day; and there's the laddies' stockings near through, and your faither's tae, and the whole work o' the house left to me; 'deed it's no richt o' ye, Nanny. Gin ye were ill, there's naething I wouldna dae for ye; but it's no that, but just the nonsense that May Hislop has been telling you about the grand doings in Edinbro', that's made ye discontented wi' your ain hame and folks."

"No, mither," the girl said, "that's no the reason; but I *want* to go. The quiet here

wearies me ; and if only faither and you would let
me go, by-and-by I'd come back again and maybe
settle down ; now, I canna ;" and the girl burst
into tears.

Mrs. Duncan was a hard-working woman, and
in her own way proud of her only daughter, now
eighteen years old, and the eldest of a family of
six ; five sturdy boys kept the hands of mother
and daughter busy repairing and making garments.
But till lately Nanny had been the blithest of
lassies, quick at her needle, and ever ready with
hand and head to serve the other members of the
family. She was a favourite, too, in the castle,
where she would now and then be sent for to do
a day's work when visitors were there; and she,
like many of the other cottagers around, looked up
with reverence to the old lady and Miss Hannah,
and accepted silently the few words of good advice
upon the virtue of modesty which the latter lady
made a point of addressing to the young people
resident on the estate.

But a change had come over the girl : work was
neglected, her merry laugh had ceased, and a
weary spirit of discontent had come over her,
making her listen eagerly to the account a companion had given her of the attraction of a town
life ; and so, from some cause or other, Nanny

Duncan, instead of being the comfort and pride of her parents' hearts, had become a source of misery to them.

Only once, for weeks, had Nanny appeared to take any interest in the bits of news that her father was sure to bring from the castle of the doings there; and that was when he had told how the young wife was sorely cast down by her husband's sudden departure, adding his own idea, that Miss Hannah would have borne it far more bravely if she had been in her place.

Then Nanny raised her head from her stocking, and said indignantly, " But, faither, we canna blame the young leddy for being wae; it maun be sair, sair for her to pairt frae her husband, gin she lo'ed him;" adding in a lower tone, as if speaking to herself, " besides, I misdoubt if Miss Hannah could lo'e onybody ower weel, she's sae cold like."

Nanny had as yet never seen the young lady save at a distance; but the accounts she had heard from the other servants of her beauty and gentleness, made her wonder how her father had taken what seemed like a dislike to her; and ever since the captain's departure the girl, in her own heart, had felt sorely for the young wife.

The evening of the day we write of, Duncan had returned home tired, and more than usually silent. He missed his girl's blithe welcome, and was secretly chafing at her desire to leave her home and seek change of scene. All day he had been out of humour, feeling himself a tried man, and obeying orders sulkily; refusing, even at the laird's desire, to allow one of the carriage horses to be taken out, saying it had been out the day before. James reigned supreme in the stable, and had done so for years; so his master, seeing his humour, thought it best to leave him alone, and leaving the stable, went to tell Edith and Hannah, who were to have driven to the post-town, that it was impossible; telling the reason, and adding, half-laughingly, to his sister-in-law, "You see, it's no use to argue the matter with James; some evil would be sure to happen to the horses if I insisted; so a wilful man must have his way. After all, it's only a chance whether we would have got a letter or not."

Great, therefore, was his surprise when, half an hour afterwards, the carriage drove up to the door, and the coachman sent to ask if the "leddies" were ready for the drive.

It was some time ere the laird heard that Edith, sorely disappointed at not being able to drive to D——, where, it was possible, she might find a letter from her husband awaiting her, had gone to the stable, and pleaded her cause with the stubborn old man. " It was mair nor mortal man could stan'," he said afterwards, " to see the tears in her young een, and hear her ask me to put mysel' in her place, and fancy hoo I wad feel. Aweel, my heart's no jist made o' stane, and sae I told her a' would be right; and if a letter was to be gotten, she wouldna hae to say James Duncan hindered her getting it a day sooner. 'Deed, sir, it's a' true that the ithers were sayin' the day. She kind o' throws a glamour ower folks. There's a hantle o' power in her."

And in his heart the laird of Oakwood acknowledged that the old man was right—round old and young the girl-wife was throwing a glamour, the source of which was love, Christian love, which subdueth stubborn hearts, and softens hard ones. She was silently yet surely storming ancient, time-hardened strongholds; but the weapons she used were not carnal ones, mighty to pull down and destroy, but those of " love, joy, peace, long-suffering, gentleness, meekness, temperance, faith," which silently undermine and subdue all resisting impediments.

No wonder, therefore, that when Duncan broke a long silence as he sat, pipe in mouth, in his own cottage, his wife and daughter were amazed at his words:—"Ay, but the young leddy *has* a kindly heart. You should have seen her when she got the captain's letter the day—didna I tell ye there was a letter frae him?—and he mentions that ere he landed a battle had been fought, and, amongst others, Widow Johnstone's son Alick was killed. The minute she read it she turned to the laird, saying, 'Where does the poor woman live? Oh, I must go and see her, and break the sad news to her.' And when the laird told her he was an only child, but his mother was sae angered at his listing for a soldier that she will allow no one to name him to her, and lives alone, scarce speaking to a neighbour, she cried 'most like a bairn, she was that vexed for the poor woman. Aweel, gudewife, I'm no that proud but I can own when I have been wrong; and what I hae seen the day has shown me I was wrang about the young leddy. She has a wonderfu' gentle way wi' her; and it's my belief that if onybody can win their way to Widow Johnstone's heart, it'll be the captain's wife.

"But, Nanny," he said, as he suddenly caught sight of his daughter's face, "what ails ye? Ye look maist as white as a ferlie. O lassie! can ye no tell your ain faither and mither what's wrang wi' ye?"

Nanny, thus accosted, sprang to her feet. "It's naething, faither; jist the heat. I'll slip out a bit, and get the air. Never you heed me, mither; I'll be back in no time."

Once in the fresh air, her strength, which had almost failed her, came back; and she walked quickly on through the glen, where the moon-beams were already silvering the stream. Across a rustic wooden bridge she went, hardly seeming to note anything around her, though her steps startled the rabbit in the woods, and roused some of the birds from their early sleep. Still she went on and on, till she left the glen behind her, and reached a solitary cottage which stood on a little knoll. Close to the cottage the girl crept stealthily, as if fearing observation, and then peered in through the small window. By the flickering light of the fire she saw the form of an old woman, seated with her head leaning on her hands, rocking herself to and fro, as if in an agony of spirit; and on the stillness of the evening air rose a heart-felt, bitter wail, "Oh, my son, my son! would God I had died for thee, my son, my son!"

Then Nanny knew that the old woman had heard the sad news. How she longed to creep in beside her and comfort her, or, if that might not be, weep with her; but she dared not. What

right had she, she asked herself, to share that
grief? though well she knew none, save his
mother, had loved the soldier lad as she had done,
since the time they went together to the parish
school, when she was a wee lassie of five years,
and he a sturdy boy of ten or more. There were
rough places on the road to be passed, but they
harmed her not, for his strong arms carried her
over them all; and when the snow-drifts lay deep,
she knew no fear, with Alick Johnstone's hand to
hold her up. And so it had always been, the
childish love between them changing to a fuller,
deeper one, as years went on. Well did they
understand each other's hearts. But a day came
when, overborne by the entreaties of a companion,
the young shepherd (for such he was) had enlisted,
and gone off to a foreign land; and the deep love
which he bore to the playmate of his childhood
remained untold, as far as words were concerned.
And so, though ever since his departure Nanny
had drooped, and grown moody, and changed, her
womanly pride forbade her telling her grief, as she
had no outward token to show that her love was
returned. As far as she was concerned, she
needed none. It needs no outward token or set
phrase of words to tell one is loved. But though
the loving actions, the thoughtful care, the looks

"WHAT IS THE MATTER TO-DAY, LITTLE WOMAN?" MR. OGILVIE
SAID KINDLY.   (Page 88).

face page 80

that expressed far more than words could have done, sufficed for herself, she knew they were as nothing to others; and if Mrs. Johnstone knew, as Nanny suspected, of her son's love for her, she was the last person to tell it, as, for some unknown cause, she had never cared for her.

Poor Nanny! she was to be pitied; she was going about bearing a heavy burden of sorrow, and as yet she knew nothing of the Great Burden-bearer, who waited only to hear her cry, "Lord, help!" to reveal himself and bring comfort to her. Her heart felt nigh to breaking as she looked at the widowed mother in her great sorrow; and compassion overcoming her fear, she opened the cottage door and boldly entered. Not a word could she speak—her very tongue seemed para-lyzed—but she threw herself at the mother's feet and wept with her; but the widow made no sign, —nay, rather repulsed the girl, and motioned her to depart. And at last she did so, leaving the mother alone with her grief,—refusing all comfort from man, and knowing nothing of the love which He whose very being she had ignored for years bore to her, and was willing to lavish on her if only she would seek it in his appointed way.

All nature looked peaceful and serene as Nanny slowly retraced her way homewards. Yet there were heavy hearts that night in that lonely district. For long, Satan had hung up before the eyes of many there a veil, to hide from them the light of the glorious gospel of Jesus Christ; but, almost unconsciously, a cry for light and help was beginning to arise. And in the hour of sorrow lips were crying, "God be pitiful!" who ne'er said, "God be praised!"

One ray of hope had entered Nanny's heart, as regarded the poor widow, ere she fell asleep. The young "leddy" might comfort her—father even had said so—and the next morning she would go to the castle and ask her to visit her. But man proposes—God disposes. When morning came, poor Nanny was tossing with fever, and unable to rise from bed. Sorely she murmured at the hard trial, yet knew not that it was to prove a messenger of mercy; and that it was a Hand of love, a pierced Hand, that laid her low.

CHAPTER VIII.

LITTLE GRETCHEN'S MISSION.

"If you cannot speak like angels,
If you cannot preach like Paul,
You can tell the love of Jesus,
You can say *he* died for all."

EARLY next morning Hannah Ogilvie was seen to go out of the castle in walking attire; a very unusual proceeding, for, as we have already seen, she considered that the morning hours should be devoted entirely to study. Her brother met her at the door, so when they assembled in the breakfast-room he alluded to her morning-walk in a playful way. Her answer chilled him.

"Yes, George, I did go out early this morning. I felt it to be my duty to do so. I wished to see that poor wayward woman, Widow Johnstone, and, if possible, to comfort her; but the ingratitude of the lower classes now-a-days is something fearful. She would not even open her door to admit me;

and when I, so to speak, forced my way in, not
one word of thanks would she give me for coming
out at such an inconvenient hour to see her ;—there
she sat, stiff and hard as a stone, not a tear falling,
not a word of acknowledgment that it was her own
fault that had caused her son's death ; for it is well
known it was her fearful temper drove the lad to
enlist. Really it was a grievous sight—no seeing
in the event the hand of Providence ; indeed, altogether, she is behaving like a heathen. But it
is all of a piece ; want of reverence for their betters,
and the insubordination of the young, are two of
the great evils of the day."

Edith's eyes filled with tears as her sister-in-law
spoke. "Oh, Hannah," she said, "perhaps the
poor woman is too miserable to speak ; all the
more so if, as you think, she had any hand in
driving away her son, her only son. Is there no
one she loves who can speak to her ? "

"No," said the laird ; "she is a strange body—
no one ever cared for her, or she for any one save
that lad. I think Hannah must be wrong in saying her temper drove him away, for to him she
was gentleness itself, and he was a good son ; but,
except him, I believe she does not care for any
human being."

As he spoke, he felt a gentle touch on his

shoulder, and, turning quickly, saw Max standing behind him. "Oh, sir," he said, "Widow Johnstone does love some one; she loves Gretchen very much, and with her she is always gentle."

"Gretchen! why, when does she see her?" said the old lady.

"You remember, ma'am, when Nurse Craig was ill about three years ago, and Gretchen was suffering so much, how you got Mrs. Johnstone to come to sit up with her at night; well, I think she learned to love her then, and she comes now and then to see her. And ever since her son went away, I've seen her cry quite softly when Gretchen asked about him; and once she said, that now that he was gone, she loved no one in the world like little Gretchen."

It was seldom that Max spoke so much in the presence of his grandmother and aunt, or even his father, but now grief for the poor lone woman loosened his tongue.

Yes; of course, all remembered how Mrs. Johnstone had helped to tend Gretchen, but no one knew she had cared for her, nor did they see how her so doing could mend matters now.

"We had better let the subject drop," said Hannah; "we have done our duty, and when people are obstinate nothing can win them."

"Save love," said a hollow voice.

Edith looked round to see who spoke, but she saw only the old butler, and Mr. Ross, who was saying, "Come along, Master Max, lesson-hour has come." Who then had spoken, or had she only fancied she heard the thought of her heart uttered aloud? She could not tell; but all that day, and the next also, the words rang in her ears, "Won by love," and she rested not till she found herself seated in the old woman's cottage; and after an hour of what seemed unavailing talk, whilst on her knees asking Him who, whilst He tarried on earth, bore such a loving heart to the sorrowing ones, and who comforted the widowed mother of Nain, to come Himself and speak peace to this suffering, childless widow, she felt a hot tear fall on her clasped hands, and one sob after another of bitter anguish struck her ear. The ice was broken; the poor mother wept like a child. "Love had conquered."

Bitter, bitter were the days of grief that followed, but they were no longer hopeless ones. The widow had become as a little child, and thankfully she valued the kindness lavished on her. Now no neighbour was refused admittance, but to them she spoke not of her sorrow; only to her young "leddy" would she do that. "She could feel for her," said she;

"she too had a loved one in a distant land exposed to all the dangers of war; but even if her husband were to fall in battle she would have no remorse —it wasnae her hand had driven him there." But when Edith sought to get her to tell her how she had done that, she would again become reserved. Once after such a question she looked wildly round and asked why Nanny Duncan never came to see her; adding, "Ay, but she did come ane nicht; I saw her: but it was in my dream, I think; *she* would ne'er come here." Who, then, was Nanny? queried Edith; but she got no response, only a bewildered look, which made her afraid the old woman's reason was going.

Day after day found Edith a visitor in the lonely cottage, and eagerly were her visits looked for. Many a holy word of love and peace was spoken there. Often was Jesus held up as the way, the truth, and the life; but though the widow listened, and loved to listen, to the story of the Cross, it was not Edith's hand, all loving as it was, that was commissioned to lead that sorrowing soul there, where alone she could find peace; it was a child's one was to lead her to Jesus. Little Gretchen had a mission of high honour intrusted to her, and the hand that had only a few weeks before touched for herself the hem of the Saviour's garment was the one to bring the sorrowing woman in contact with it also. Now, as of old, the Lord's strength is made perfect in weakness, and out of the mouths of babes and sucklings is perfected praise.

Mr. Ogilvie, true to the resolution he had formed some time before, of taking the ascendency in regard to his children's upbringing, and letting the spirit of love mingle with the strict discipline of their grandmother's training, now often entered the play-room, and spent some time by Gretchen's couch. The tenderest love of father and child was springing up between them.

One morning, on Mr. Ogilvie entering unobserved, he was grieved to find Gretchen in tears. "What is the matter to-day, little woman?" he said kindly, seating himself beside her; "is the pain worse? or has Aunt Hannah inflicted too long a lesson?"

"No, father, it is none of these things; only I want, oh so much! to be able to walk; then I could go to see Widow Johnstone, for I love her very dearly, and she is too ill to come to see me. Father, could I go? Don't you remember, when Uncle Jack was married, and they lit the bonfire on the hill, how I was carried on a litter a long way to see it?—and even grandmamma said it did no harm. Oh, do say I may try."

The little pleader in her excitement crept very

close to her father, and nestled her fair curly head
on his breast ; and with those soft blue eyes, so like
her dead mother's, gazing into his with their im-
ploring look, he could not say her nay.

So, with the aid of the coachman and Max, little
Gretchen was conveyed to the cottage, and laid by
the side of the childless widow.   What words
passed between them we know not ; we believe,
however, not many were spoken, nor were they
needed.   "To help and to heal a sorrow love and
silence are always best ;" but of one thing we are
sure, that as the angels that night heard the voice
of the old woman raised in penitent and believing
prayer in the name of Jesus, they rejoiced with
great joy, and with their song mingled one which
rose from a little girl on a couch of suffering, whose
child-words of love the Lord had used to point the
aged widow to the cross of Jesus.

Soon after Gretchen's visit the widow rose from
her bed, and once more began her daily work,
chastened, but yet rejoicing.   She had lost a child,
but she had found a Saviour, and from henceforth
she lived no more to herself, but to Him who had
redeemed her.   Love, "the love which passeth all
understanding," had won the citadel of her heart,
and reigned there.

And when next Gretchen lay under the old oaks

she too had a new song on her lips, of praise to
God, who chooseth the weak things of the world
to work his will. And she still felt as if the dear
old trees understood her joy and participated in it;
and when she whispered this belief to her Aunt
Edith, she did not smile at her childish faith, but
reminded her gently of the One who made the old
oaks to grow, and who shares all the joys of his
children.

CHAPTER IX.

THE SECRET DISCLOSED.

"O God, we come
Humbly to thee, though lips are dumb.
Tears! this is grief *they* come not nigh;
For hearts bleed most when tears are dry.
But thou dost know
The dumb, dumb grief, the aching woe.
This darkness is too dark for prayer;
But thou dost know, and thou wilt care."

MANY days had passed since Nanny Duncan had on the moonlight night taken her way through the glen to the widow's cottage, with the vain hope of gaining admittance, and if not able to comfort her, at least to be allowed to weep with her. How she was repulsed, we know; and ever since then she had been tossing on a bed of fever, now delirious, now half unconscious from very weakness. Watching by her sick-bed, the mother had learned the secret of her love; and the weary change of the last few months, the longing for different scenes, all were explained

now.   But as Mrs. Duncan knew not if that deep
love was in truth returned, with her womanly pride
and instinct she resolved to guard the secret only
revealed in the hours of delirium: for it should
never be said that a daughter of hers gave her love
to any man unsought; but all the more did the
mother's heart yearn over her suffering child.

The village doctor had been early sent for, and
every needful comfort was daily supplied from the
castle; but as it was feared the fever might prove
infectious, none of the inmates entered the cottage,
though the laird himself came every morning to
hear tidings of the suffering girl. And loving-
hearted little Gretchen shed tears when Nurse
Craig told her how the young girl, who had often
slipped up to the nursery when she was at the
castle, was lying insensible on her sick-bed. And
Gretchen did more than shed tears of pity—she
told the Saviour she had learned to love all about
the sick girl, and asked his aid to heal and bless:
and it was from Gretchen's lips that Widow Johnstone first heard of Nanny's illness. Little did the
child understand the cause of the deadly pallor
that spread over the old woman's face, or the
meaning of the words that fell with such a bitterness of remorse from her lips: "She too, she too!
God have mercy on me, and spare her life!"

But that night, when poor Mrs. Duncan was preparing, almost exhausted, to sit up again and watch by the sick-bed, to the surprise of herself and husband the door was gently opened, and the widow walked in, quietly greeting the inmates, and making tender inquiries about Nanny. She announced her intention of remaining, if she were allowed, and watching by the sufferer. Eagerly the father accepted the kind offer, as he felt his wife was worn out, and sorely needed rest herself. And so it turned out that, when the gray light of a September morning dawned on the little cottage, Nanny Duncan opened her eyes to see the childless widow sitting beside her; and the first words that met her ear, on her returning consciousness, were the ones, " Forgive me, my poor girl, forgive!"

For many days after that, Nanny's life still hung on a thread; but, by God's blessing on the careful nursing she received, whilst the autumnal colouring still lingered on the trees, and the glen glistened in tints of amber, russet, and gold, strength began slowly to return.

She was sitting up one day, carefully protected from the cold. Her mother had left her on an errand—almost the first time since her illness; so Nanny was alone. And yet not alone, for a new joy had entered her heart during those weary hours

of convalescence.   Jesus had revealed himself to
the sorrow-stricken girl, and his blessed invitation
to the weary and heavy-laden soul had met with a
hearty response.   In her conscious moments, it
was Widow Johnstone's voice reading the words of
love that fell on her ear, and first awoke a desire
to know for herself more of that message of peace
and joy ; and as is so often the case, the one who
had but begun to climb the heavenly ladder was
the one commissioned to help the soul that still
stood wavering to begin to climb likewise.   It was
of these things that Nanny was thinking as she sat
alone.   Her heart was sad still as she thought she
would never see on earth again the loved face, or
hear the to her dear voice, of the young shepherd,
Alick Johnstone.   Oh, if only she had had one
word from his lips or his pen, one token to tell he
had loved her—that she had more than an old
companion's right to weep over his early death, his
nameless grave !   But she had none, and she knew
not even her mother had, in her moments of delirium, guessed her secret.   But she had now one
Friend to whom she could tell all her griefs, and
who, she felt, could whisper peace to her even as
he had done to the desolate widow.   As she
mused, the door opened, and Widow Johnstone
entered, pleased to find the sick girl so far recovered.

Nanny gave her a hearty welcome. These two had learned to love each other ; and yet on the subject nearest to their hearts no words had passed. But now the ice broke. It was the widow who spoke :—

"Nanny, forgive me. I have sinned sorely agin thee, my puir bairn. Look here !" And with her head bent low, and tears fast falling, she placed a letter in the girl's hand. "He gave it me," she said, "the nicht he went awa'—my puir dear laddie !—and he charged me to gie it to you. But I never did. In it, Nanny, you'll read aw, and ken noo how dearly he looed you. And it was me, his ain mother, who held him back, and told him my curse would rest on his head if ever he married you. Na, lassie, dinna look so hard on me. I ken noo how wicked I was ; and oh, may you never thole the pain I suffer, for it was my hand drave him awa' ! He was weel content to hae spent his life here, as his faither had afore him ; but without you he couldna bide, and he was too good a son to marry wi' his widowed mother's curse on him. Sae he went, and my heart seemed to turn to stane ; and I hated the very sicht o' you. And noo my sin has found me out, and the Lord has taken the light o' my heart frae me. Nanny Duncan, say you forgie me !"

Not long was that forgiveness withheld. Through hot bitter tears, Nanny's heart was full of joy. She knew now how fully, how deeply she had been loved. She had a right now that none could question to mourn over the early death of the soldier lad ; a right to fill, as far as she could, a daughter's place to his sorrowing mother. And the tears these two mingled together that autumn day, united their hearts in a bond that was " unto death "—a double bond, in the earthly love which both felt for the dead, and the heavenly love which had arisen in their dark hearts, and made them one in Christ Jesus.

Once more there were peace and happiness in the little cottage, for Nanny was her own self again,— only far gentler and better, her father said, with a softened look in her face, and a higher purpose and aim in her life. And even in the castle the rumour ran that Nanny Duncan, like the Widow Johnstone, had become a changed person : and when little Gretchen heard it, she smiled her happy smile now, and pointing to her Aunt Edith, said, " It's all her doings, though she knows it not. Nanny, too, has been ' won by love '—the love of God which is in Christ Jesus."

CHAPTER X.

THE BABY GIRL.

"God's gift of purest blessing,
Full little cup of bliss!
No gift of gold or jewels
Could be so dear as this."

THE daylight of a February morning had begun to dawn, and a crimson flush was rising in the eastern horizon, proclaiming the advent of the sun, slightly colouring the snow, which lay thick around Oakwood Castle, and glimmering on the silvery, mossy covering of the now leafless oak-trees, when Max stepped into little Gretchen's room. The child was sitting up in bed, as if in eager expectation, even as she had sat for more than an hour. "Now!" she exclaimed eagerly, "O Max, tell me! what is it? Why has nurse remained away so long, and what is the secret she said she would tell me soon?"

At these words Max knelt down beside his

sister, and with a soft light in his gray eyes, said, "Gretchen, God has given Aunt Edith a little baby girl."

How Gretchen's face brightened! "O Max, is it possible? How happy she will be! A baby— only think! When may I see it? I can hardly believe it. Why, Max, it is almost as good as if God had given us a little sister, is it not? Won't Uncle Jack be glad when he hears! I do so wonder what it is like!"

Gretchen heard that sooner than she expected, and from the lips of the last person she would have expected to do so; for even as she spoke Aunt Hannah came into the room, pale and tired like, and lame still from the effect of a bad accident which she had met with, and which had confined her to her couch for the last three months. "Yes, children," she said, "Aunt Edith has got a dear little baby girl, the very image of herself, with dark eyes and black hair. You shall see it, Gretchen, as soon as you can. But in the meantime you must both be as still and quiet as possible."

Gretchen could scarcely believe it was Aunt Hannah who spoke, so softened, so changed was her voice and appearance. Had she seen her as she entered her own room, and heard her return thanks to God for life spared and life given, she would have wondered still more. For, for nearly three months the children had hardly seen their aunt, and knew nothing of the softening process which she had undergone. Hannah Ogilvie's was no sudden conversion—no marvellous change of nature : not in a moment had the hard crust of self which had entwined her heart yielded. No ; long, patient, self-denying forbearance had Edith to exercise, not only daily, but moment by moment, ere the heart of her sister-in-law softened towards her ; and longer yet had she to wait ere she saw that heart yield to a higher power.

It happened thus : One autumn day, when Edith was returning from a walk to the coachman's cottage, and had gone down the glen a little way, and stooped to gather some of the bright-coloured rose-hips, which hung in clusters over the little rivulet, she heard a cry of pain, and to her surprise saw Hannah lying at the foot of the steep bank unable to move. Walking quickly along, her foot had slipped, and she had fallen. And when, by Edith's exertions, assistance was got and she was carried home, it was discovered her right limb was broken ; and the doctor at once told her she would be confined to her couch for weeks to come. During those weeks Edith tended her sister-in-law with

the most patient love; repulsed again and again,
she still persevered, letting love shine forth in all
her actions, and seeking strength for her work
from the Lord Jesus. Whilst Hannah was feverish
and restless, she watched beside her, and even
(when Mrs. Ogilvie would allow her) sat up for
hours at night. Little enough thanks she got for
her trouble; but she worked for no earthly reward.
And sometimes, when rumours of battles reached
the castle, and the young wife's heart beat with
fear, she would spend some portion of the night
watches in prayer. And once, whilst so engaged,
and her tears were gently falling, Hannah awoke,
and her ear caught her own name, as Edith pled
with the Lord that her pain might be relieved,
and that the Holy Spirit might touch her heart.
The next day, to Edith's great amazement and
joy, she called her to her and kissed her, though
without saying a word. But from that hour a
softening was visible; and even the old lady
began to see that Hannah's eyes looked wist-
fully towards the door if Edith were absent longer
than usual. And when the Laird of Oakwood
entered his sister's room he was startled to see
a gentler expression on her face than it had ever
worn; and the voice that asked if Gretchen was
pretty well just now, was so unlike that of his

sister Hannah, that he started, and almost fancied such a change must be a token of approaching death.

Yes ; the " love that suffers long, that beareth much, that is ever kind, and that meekly suffers many a wrong, though sore with hardships pressed," as evinced in the daily life by a child of God, was made the means of opening the long-closed heart to the wonderful, patient love of Him whom for so long she had kept standing outside the door of her heart, yea till " his head was filled with the dew, and his hair with the drops of the night." But at last the cry met his all-hearing ear, " Enter!" and he entered, and at his presence the darkness fled and light shone. And with the spirit of a little child the once proud, self-satisfied Hannah Ogilvie seated herself, like Mary of old, at the feet of Jesus, and chose the good part which could never be taken from her.

And when, after her recovery, she had to watch through long hours of suffering by Edith's bed, it was she who first received the little helpless babe into her arms, and who pressed the fondest kiss on the young mother's brow.

And whilst Edith's heart was silently thanking her loving Father in heaven for the double gift he had given her in the little daughter and the love

of her sister-in-law, Nurse Craig was inwardly
wondering at the change wrought in the proud
Miss Hannah,—a change as wonderful, she told
her old friend and confidant Thomas, as ever was
wrought on any human being. "Talk o' miracles
after that! The power that could soften a heart
like Miss Hannah's could do a' things."

"Yes, indeed, Mrs. Craig," said the old man,
"the power that has wrought the change can effect
wonders. Who save he that formed the heart can
by the power of the Holy Spirit renew it? You
have no forgotten the words o' the Shorter Catechism, Agnes, that we learned when we were
bairns, that 'effectual calling is the work of God's
Spirit, whereby, convincing us of our sin and
misery, enlightening our minds in the knowledge
of Christ, and renewing our wills, he doth persuade
and enable us to embrace Jesus Christ, freely
offered to us in the gospel.' Ay, *that's* the power
that has wrought the change in mair hearts than
one in this old castle. But the instrument the
Lord has used through which to work has been
ane like unto an angel we have entertained unawares."

Great was the joy amongst many of the cottagers
when they heard of the birth of the little baby,
who had come to cheer the heart of one who, by

her gentleness and love, had won all their hearts
and the tears of mothers fell fast as they thought
of its father in a far-away land, exposed to all the
dangers of a deadly war. And when Widow
Johnstone came to see the little stranger, she
clasped it to her breast, with an earnest prayer
that God would preserve its father, and bring him,
ere very long, home to his wife and little one.

When spring days came round, and violets and
primroses dotted the ground, and the young leaves
on the old oaks were being gently wooed forth by
the sun, it was a pretty sight to see little Gretchen
lying once more under their shade, with baby
beside her, its little head resting on her shoulder,
whilst its mamma watched over both, and Gretchen
and she sang together hymns of love and hope as
baby's lullaby. And the spring breezes gently
shook the quivering leaflets above them, and wafted
around the words which told of "Jesus and his
love." And through all, Gretchen still held that
the "old oaks" already knew and loved the little
baby, and whispered in its ear stories which one
day, said Gretchen, it would recall. And the old
trees all the while seemed to answer back the
child's fancies, and spread caressingly their opening
leaves over the little helpless, much-loved baby;
and the blithe little birds overhead trilled out the

spring joy of their hearts, as if they too knew all about the delights of the baby girl, and wished with their sweet songs to cheer the heart of the young mother on days when she felt sad and full of longing for her absent husband.

CHAPTER XI.

COUSIN KARL.

> In God's great field of labour
>   All work is not the same;
> He hath a service for each one
>   Who loves his holy name.
> And you to whom the secrets
>   Of all sweet sounds are known,
> Rise up! for he hath called you
>   To a mission of your own."

"MAX, Max! take care, my boy! where are you going so quickly with my precious little Rosebud?" said Edith Ogilvie, as one summer day she met her nephew carrying baby out of doors, and walking faster than her maternal fears deemed prudent.

"Never fear, Aunt Edith; baby is as safe as possible in my arms. I am taking her to Gretchen 'under the old oaks.' I have got such a famous piece of news to tell Gretchen, and she's sure to wish baby to hear all about it: she'll understand just as much as the old oaks, you know," said the boy with a merry laugh.

And so it came to pass that Rosebud Ogilvie, as she was called, was deposited on Gretchen's couch under the old oaks, and heard the grand news which Max had to impart to his sister Gretchen.

"Guess who's coming?"

Gretchen's colour rose, and half rising on her couch, she said, "O Max, is it Uncle Jack? How glad Aunt Edith will be!"

Max's countenance fell. "No, no, it is not Uncle Jack; and perhaps after all you will not care so much—it is Cousin Karl Heine, from Germany, the great musician; you know papa told me all about him. And how I have longed to see him and hear him play on the organ; and now, only to think of his coming to this old castle, and playing on *my* organ! O Gretchen, won't you be glad too? And the best of all is, Mr. Ross told me papa has asked him here just to hear me play, and judge if I may be allowed to really study music."

Gretchen's eyes shone now. "How good of papa, Max! And I am glad about Cousin Karl too; only, you see, at first I was a little disappointed. I made so sure it would be Uncle Jack; and then how happy Aunt Edith would have been!"

And Cousin Karl did come; and such a plea-

sant visitor he proved, so good-humoured and
agreeable—courteous enough to please the old
lady, and learned enough to suit Hannah, and
gentle as a woman with Gretchen and Rosebud.
As for Max, the boy was in a fairy-land of delight;
for hours he would sit entranced, listening to the
master music his cousin poured forth from the
organ. Never had he imagined such exquisite
beauty of sound and touch. And Karl, on his
part, was equally delighted with Max. The first
day he listened to the boy's strange medley of
music—now sad, now dreamy—reproducing every
emotion of his soul, Karl Heine somewhat hastily
left the room, and sought for Mr. Ogilvie. He
found him outside; and almost rushing up to him,
he put his hand on his shoulder, and, in his own
rich language, said,—

" George Ogilvie, thank God for the gift he has
given your son. Max is a born genius, all untaught as he is, unfinished in touch and composi-
tion. I am beside him but as a babe. The very
soul of music, and the aspiration of a noble nature,
wells out in his weird, wonderful compositions.
You must let him give himself up at once to the
study of music. I must take him to Germany
with me; and if he live, ere many years pass he
will have made a name in the world: and, if I

mistake not, he will put his rare gift to no mean use, but render back the gift to the Giver, and praise him with it.   And Gretchen, too, what a rich sweet voice and true ear she possesses !   Whilst I remain here, I mean, with your leave, to instruct her also."

And so it came to pass that ere many weeks elapsed it became known that the young Laird of Oakwood was to accompany his cousin to Germany to study the noble art of music under experienced masters.   And though Gretchen's tears fell fast when she bade her loved brother adieu, and his father's voice faltered as he asked God to bless and keep him, and every one in the household mourned over his departure, still all felt it was best ; and his father recalled the words that Mr. Ross had said to him the day they had visited the waterfall, that he believed Master Max was a musical genius.

But the old man did not live to witness his pupil's departure ; only a few weeks ere that event he had died somewhat suddenly, under the roof where he had spent so many years of his life as a conscientious teacher of father and son.   Carefully was he tended ; all that sons could have done for a father, the Laird of Oakwood and Max did for the old man, who had no relations of his own alive

to care for him.   Peaceful and patient he was during his illness—God's Word his great delight, and
prayer his chief occupation.   The new minister of
Queenshope, Mr. Murray, was a frequent and
much-valued visitor by his sick-bed ; for he was
one who had proved a true gospel minister,
"rightly dividing the word of truth," and ere his
illness Mr. Ross and he had become firm friends.

But shortly ere his death the old man had
begged a special interview with Mrs. Jack Ogilvie,
and, somewhat to Edith's surprise, had told her
that it was her simple words spoken to the children about Jesus, the first night she left her room
after her husband's departure, which had touched
his heart, and led him to recall many precious
lessons taught him in his early days by a godly
mother, but which had been long forgotten.   That
very night, he went on to say, found him on his
knees, with the prayer of the publican on his lips ;
and after a dark struggle of weeks, peace through
the blood of Jesus filled his heart.   And now he
was going home, trusting not to his own merits,
but to those of Jesus.   " Yes, dear young lady,"
he said, " the Lord has blessed and is still blessing
you here, not only by your words, but by your *life*
of patience, love, and forbearance.   Go on in the
Lord's strength to tell of the love of Jesus, who

died instead of us.   It was his wonderful love, and
not the terrors of the law, that broke down my
cold heart.   It is Satan's work to go about telling
men that God hates them.   Be it yours to tell
them rather that ' God *so* loved the world, that he
gave his only begotten Son, that *whosoever* believ-
eth in him should not perish, but have everlasting
life.' "

That night the old man slept in Jesus ; and, as
the wind amongst the old oaks seemed to sing the
requiem of a ransomed soul, did Edith Ogilvie
regret the sacrifice of her wishes which she had
made in remaining, during her husband's absence,
at the Castle of Oakwood ?

It was by the death-bed of his old teacher that
the Laird of Oakwood learned many solemn lessons.   And then was the time that the mist that
had hid Jesus from his eyes for so many years fell
from them, and he saw that no outward form, no
mere circumcision of the flesh, can save a soul ;
and he too told Mr. Ross that it was Edith's words
and life of love that had first shown him what real
Christ-like religion was.

And Max, too, as he wept over the dead body
of the tutor he had always reverenced, felt his
soul more filled with the realities of eternity than
he ever had done before.   Life was so bright be-

fore him at that time, it was well that just then
his first near acquaintance with death should be
made, not to render his bright life gloomy, but to
whisper in his inmost heart the reminder, " This is
not your rest." And, on the eve of his departure,
as he sat with a very full heart beside Gretchen,
as she lay on her couch, and Aunt Edith sat be
side them speaking sweet words of love and cheer,
the boy's lips opened more than, on such a subject,
they had ever done; and he left a sweet hope
behind him, as he went forth to fight the battle of
life, that he too had enlisted in the army of the
Great King, whose leader is Jesus, the Captain of
our salvation.

And so he was off at last; and brave little
Gretchen forced back her tears, and in spirit rejoiced that it was so, even though her heart ached
with a sense of loneliness, and it was days ere her
full sweet voice was heard singing under the old
oaks, which were already putting on their brightly-
coloured autumnal garments.

CHAPTER XII.

GRETCHEN'S CLASS.

" Sing to the little children,
  And they will listen well ;
Sing grand and holy music,
  For they can feel its spell. "

SLOWLY the months rolled by ; winter's
snow and spring's green livery had both
in their season once again clothed the old
oaks with their own peculiar beauty, and
summer sunshine was once more flooding the world
with its golden beauty, even as it had done two
years before, when Edith Ogilvie came to Oakwood Castle a happy bride.   And yet, though the
relentless wheels of Time sped on, there were no
tidings of the young officer's return.   Battle after
battle had been fought, and yet the deadly war
was not ended.   Days there were, and not a few,
when Edith's heart turned sick with hope deferred.
Week after week found her hoping for her husband's speedy return, but in vain.   Oh ! in her

soul patience was to have its perfect work ; and in
the midst of her sorrow she did not give way to
idle grieving. She had found work to do for her
Lord in many ways, and been blessed in it. And
rich in the love of all hearts now in the old castle,
and devoted as she was to little Rosebud, could
she well, she asked herself, give way to discontent
or repining ? Already the little baby girl had
learned to lisp the words " mamma" and " papa ;"
and strange though it seemed, to no one, save her
mother, was the little child so attached as to Aunt
Hannah ! Truly Rosebud had been to her a very
blessing. It was the first real love that Hannah
had ever experienced ; and like all love of whatever
kind, when once it

" Took up the harp of life it struck on all its chords with might,—
Struck the chord of self, which, trembling, passed in music out of sight."

To amuse baby, Hannah's most difficult problems
and most interesting studies were cheerfully laid
aside ; and with the little one nestling in her arms,
or trotting by her side with a firm hold of her
hand, none who had not known her in days gone
by could have believed she had ever been cold,
proud, haughty, and selfish.

But there were changes going on in the quiet
neighbourhood. Time never leaves all unchanged,

and one or two important events had taken place.
One, that was exciting much interest in the castle,
was a marked improvement in Gretchen's health.
When the July days came round, Gretchen no
longer lay always on her couch; but, half sup-
ported by her father, could now and then walk
across the room, and bear without pain a drive in
the old-fashioned carriage.   Some months previous
to that time, Mr. Murray, the minister of Queenshope, had been seeing Gretchen; and hearing from
her father the nature and cause of her illness, had
told him that the very next week his uncle, a phy-
sician in London, famed for his skill in just such
cases as Gretchen's, was coming to pay him a visit
of some duration, as the state of his health made
rest absolutely necessary.   And so, in God's providence, it happened that the skilful doctor saw
little Gretchen, and at once undertook her case,
which he by no means considered a hopeless one.
The treatment at first was trying and painful, but
Gretchen in her suffering times had now an
Almighty Friend to help and sustain her, and the
very hope of being able to walk enabled her to
bear up and endure; and now the reward was
coming, and the summer days saw her gaining
strength.   The lameness would likely always remain slightly; the doctor said, but that to Gret-

chen seemed of small moment. Oh, how glad she
was, when she could write to Max and tell him
she had actually walked from one room to another!

And Gretchen's education was now carried on
regularly by Aunt Hannah, who found her pupil
an apt, attentive one, eager to get information on
all subjects, and a diligent preparer of stated
tasks. Gretchen had profited much by the singing lessons given her in the autumn by her Cousin
Karl, and had already, with her grandmother and
father's full consent, begun to turn her talent to
account. On the Sabbath evening the motherless
child might be seen seated with a group of the
cottage children around her, reading to them words
from the Book of Life, and teaching them to sing
the sweet songs of Zion. And on the summer
evenings the meetings were held under the old
oaks, and the grown sisters of the children, and
now and then the mothers, who came to take the
little ones home, would join the group and mingle
their voices in the hymn of praise, and listen to
the gospel message of peace and love; and then,
in the gray twilight of the long summer days,
stroll home through the glens and over the hills,
thanking God for the blessed change he had
wrought in the hearts of many in Oakwood Castle,

lonely cottage, and sing her sweet hymns to the dying woman.

The village doctor, when questioned as to the cause of Widow Johnstone's illness, said he could hardly tell ; but the neighbours would shake their heads and say they knew, if he did not.   She was dying of a broken heart : and I believe it was even so.

CHAPTER XIII.

EVENTIDE.

" Home—light—home ! the light of a cloudless day,
  It breaks o'er the city whose builder is God, and never shall fade away;
  Nor sun, nor moon, nor stars o'er the mansions of rest may reign;
  For the Lamb is the light of that golden land—the light is the Lamb
    once slain."

AN oppressively hot summer day was drawing to a close when Nanny Duncan rose
from her post of close watching by the
death-bed of the poor widow, and stood
outside the cottage to breathe the sweet
air which the evening breezes were beginning to
stir. It was a Sabbath even, but Nanny's duty
had kept her away that day from the house of
God. Very peaceful was the whole scene before
her. Everything around spoke of rest from labour : the half-cut fields of corn, the unused imple-
ments of labour, the hard-worked horses quietly
grazing, all brought to Nanny's remembrance the
rest of the day of which it is written, " God ended

his work which he had made ; and he *rested* on the
seventh day......and God blessed the seventh day,
and sanctified it." And her thoughts turned to
words spoken some hours before by the young
lady, of the higher joy which believers now have
on their day of rest, in rejoicing in a risen Lord,
whose resurrection from the dead told of atone-
ment accepted, of victory won ; yes, because he
lives, his people shall live also. And thinking of
her loved one in his distant grave, and the poor
dying woman so soon to put off this mortal body,
Nanny began to ponder over the question asked
so long ago : " How shall the dead be raised, and
with what body shall they come ? " She hardly
cared to answer it even to herself. One day she
would certainly know ; till then, to her it would
be as difficult to explain the way as it would be to
tell how the grains of the corn she had seen sown
in the earth months before were now changed into
the rich golden fields before her. One thing only
she grasped by faith,—that, in the words of the
Catechism, learned so early by every Scottish
child, " at the resurrection, believers, being raised
up in glory, shall be openly acknowledged and
acquitted in the day of judgment, and made per-
fectly blessed in the full enjoyment of God to all
eternity." Yes, that was enough for her ; then

she would meet those loved ones who slept in Jesus, and for whom her heart now ached so sorely.

But no longer could she stand musing there; twilight was stealing slowly over the hills, and she feared the sick woman might have awoke and required her. Ere she turned in she looked down the valley in the direction of her home, to see if her father were coming, as he had promised to do, in the gloaming. In the far distance she thought she descried him, but was not certain; it might only be the figure of one of the shepherds returning from his evening visit to his flock on the hills.

She found the patient still asleep, and opening the large Bible that lay on the small table, she turned to the fifteenth chapter of First Corinthians, and began to study what the Word of God says on the subject she had been musing on. She read on for some time, and was so absorbed in thought that she never raised her head when the door softly opened, and a man's step echoed on the floor. She heard it notwithstanding, and thinking it was her father, said quietly, without turning round, "Father, she's asleep." A hand was laid on her shoulder, and a voice—not that of her father, but of one she never thought to have heard again on earth—said, "Nanny!" She gave no cry.

She sought to say a name, but no words would come; her face had turned ashen white—every limb was trembling—another moment, and she would have fallen to the ground; but a strong arm was thrown around her, and the loved voice of the young soldier, Alick Johnstone, was soothing her with words of fondest affection and love!

Was she dreaming, she asked herself, as her half-suspended consciousness returned, or was this all a reality? A movement in the bed roused her; she felt she must act, and quickly; for should the widow's eye rest on her son, the sudden shock would be death. Quietly she drew him out of the room, and in a few hurried words told him of his mother's state, and also that she as well as herself had believed him to be dead.

"But, Nanny," he queried, "how comes it that I find you here tending my mother—you whom she despised so much? My poor mother—have I returned only to find her dying?"

There was no time for further talk; a low voice was heard calling on Nanny, and signing to the soldier to remain where he was, the girl went to the bedside.

"Nanny," the widow said, "I have had a strange dream. I thought I was one of the party at the gate of the city of Nain, that the young leddy read

to us about this morning; and I dreamed I was
the widowed mother who was following her son
to the grave, only it was soldiers who were carrying the bier; and I heard like the sound of a
muffled drum, for it was a soldier lad we were
carrying to burial. Then, just as we came to the
gate, Jesus met us; and, as we read in Scripture,
he stopped us, and hearing the dead man was the
only son of his mother, and she was a widow, he
turned to me and said, 'Weep not;' then he
touched the bier, and said to my son, 'Young man,
arise!' and he brought him to me, and I felt his
arms around my neck, and I woke. And, Nanny,
listen to me, and say not my mind is wandering,
but I *saw* my son Alick standing in the gloamin'
yonder, and I heard his voice; but whilst I looked
he slowly vanished from my eyes. I believe it
was his spirit, and he's been sent to call me home."

Nanny's tears were her only answer. "Nay,
mother" (the name by which she now addressed
the widow), "it was no spirit you saw; the Lord's
power and his love are as great now as when he
tarried on earth. Alick lives! I too have seen
him, and talked with him. Mother, could ye bear
to see him, and yet see a sad change?"

One other moment and Alick Johnstone was
clasped in his mother's arms, the past all forgotten

in that moment of joy. "Now, Lord, let thy servant depart in peace," were the widow's first words.

But the mother's eye, quicker even in death than that of others, descried sooner than Nanny's had done that her strong stalwart lad had lost an arm. Sorely wounded, unto death as many had thought, he had been found on the field of battle and removed by kind friends to a little cottage, where for weeks, nay months, he had lain between life and death; his left arm had at once been amputated, and his numerous wounds brought him to the very gates of death. But on that bed of sickness thoughts of eternity had filled his heart, and the Bible given to him on board ship by a Christian officer became his greatest comfort and joy. There he read of the way of salvation through faith in Christ Jesus, of which the same officer had often spoken to him, and to which at the time he had paid little attention; but in these silent suffering hours the Holy Spirit opened his heart to receive Jesus as his own personal Saviour. Often his thoughts turned to his widowed parent, whom, he felt, he should not have left despite the injustice she had done him; and, through all, his heart beat fondly and truly to the young girl he loved so dearly, and again in the foreign land he seemed in dreams to be wandering with her through the glens and over the hills of his native land. Many a time had he prayed that she and his mother also might know the Saviour he had learned to love, and listen to his voice saying, " Come unto me, and I will give you rest." And now he found that, even whilst he had been praying thus, the answer had come.

Very quickly did the news spread of the return of the widow's son, who had for so long been mourned for as dead ; and nowhere was the news received with greater joy than in the castle. Not long did the young wife withhold her heartfelt congratulation, as she hastened to the cottage to hear from the soldier's lips the account of many wonderful escapes, and to join the dying woman in her prayer of thanksgiving. And when, ere her death, the mother joined the hands of Nanny and her son, and, making them kneel beside her bed, asked God to forgive her for all the misery she had caused them, and to bless them and be their God and Saviour all the days of their lives, it was Edith's voice that, when the old woman's broke down, took up the strain, and rendered thanks for the love which had won the hearts of all the little group—even the love of God in Christ Jesus.

And when shortly afterwards the widow breathed

her last on the breast of her son, it was Edith
Ogilvie who, amidst the sobs of all in that room,
returned thanks to God for another soul safe for
ever in the arms of Jesus.   And tears not a few
were shed by Gretchen when Edith told her that
the poor woman whom she loved so much had
fallen asleep in Jesus; and as she thought of her
old friend now in glory joining in the song of the
redeemed, the soft sighing of the summer breeze
amongst the branches of the old oaks seemed to
her to be as a hymn of praise, low and soft, raised
by angel voices rejoicing over another jewel sparkling in the Redeemer's crown.

CHAPTER XIV.

FAREWELL TO OAKWOOD CASTLE.

> " O spotless Lamb of God! in thee
> Our Father's holiness we see;
> And with delight thy children trace
> In thee his wondrous love and grace.
>
> " For thou didst leave thy throne above
> To teach us that our ' God is love;'
> And now we see his glory shine
> In every word and deed of thine."

MONTHS had passed again; spring's budding beauties were clothing the earth, and almost merging into summer's richer glow. Hawthorn blossoms hung on the hedges, and the laburnum's golden tresses were hanging from the trees, when a quiet bridal party took their way from the old hall in the castle (where the marriage ceremony had been performed by Mr. Murray) to the old oaks, under which the marriage dinner was spread. The early summer sunshine was warm enough then, and the leaves on the old oaks were not yet so fully

out as to intercept the glow. A happy group was
collected there—the bride looking proud and happy
as she leaned on the arm of her husband, dressed
in his soldier's dress; and the old coachman's face
beams with delight as he looks at the couple, and
hears on every side whispered remarks on the
beauty of the bride: for now, as in days gone by,
Nanny was her father's pride; and despite the
want of his arm, her husband, Alick Johnstone,
was one to be pleased with.

He had obtained the situation of head shepherd
to a neighbouring laird, so Nanny in her new home
will not be far removed from the friends of her
youth; and will be still near enough to have a visit
now and then from the "leddy" she loves so much,
Mrs. Jack Ogilvie, as well as from Miss Hannah,
whom all the cottagers now have learned to love
also. Ay, and even from the laird himself! And
some day he has promised to bring Miss Gretchen,
who walks about in her bride's-maid dress saying
words of cheer to all the guests, and seeing that
all are made comfortable.

Hannah Ogilvie was there too,—no longer the
proud, unsympathizing woman, living only for self.
A softer light was in her eyes now, and a gentler
sound in her voice; and the words of advice which
she still loves to give are not only wise in them

selves, but given in a loving spirit, which makes them far more palatable. For Hannah has learned at the feet of Christ, that if we would copy his example in that as in other things, even words of rebuke must be spoken in love.

Grandmamma Ogilvie has also joined the party, leaning on her son's arm. She has aged since we first saw her receiving the young bride in the guest-room of the old castle; and though stately and stiff as of old, yet those who know her best can tell of a change in her also, not so marked as in Hannah, but yet a real change too. And we notice the softened look most when her eyes glance at the fair daughter-in-law she has learned to love so fondly; and as she looks she notes as others of the party have already done, a shade of sadness on her brow, as of one whose heart was heavy, and who yet for the sake of others strove to hide it.

And, truth to tell, more than one of the party feared Edith Ogilvie had too good cause for grief. Some months had now elapsed since she had had tidings of her husband. The last letter had spoken of a wound received shortly before he wrote; which, however, he declared to be slight. Since then news had reached England of the storming of Ciudad Rodrigo; but there was no mention either amongst casualties or otherwise of Colonel (for

9

such he now was) Jack Ogilvie. Ay, Edith
during the long waiting-time was proving the truth
of the words, "That it is through much tribulation we must enter into the kingdom." But she
was learning also the faithfulness of Him who hath
said to His people, "As thy days thy strength
shall be."

She was standing now under the old oaks, with
Rosebud at her side, addressing a pleasant word to
a timid girl who sat near, when a sudden cry from
little Rosebud—"A carriage, mamma! a carriage!"—turned every eye. And in another
moment Jack Ogilvie stood in their midst! Amid
the assembled group he looked but for one form
and saw only one face, and as all made way for
him, in a minute he had clasped his wife and child
to his heart, and the long time of separation seemed
all forgotten in the joy of that moment of reunion
under the old oaks.

There was much to tell that evening, as the
family group met in the guest-chamber, from which
neither Gretchen nor little Rosebud was excluded
now. Through much trouble and many hardships
had the young officer passed since the last evening
he had spent at Oakwood Castle; and amidst all,
as he afterwards told his wife, the Friend he had
learned to love had never left, never forsaken him;

and even when more than once death had appeared to him to be very near, he had been enabled quietly by faith to commit his wife and child into the hands of his loving Saviour.

Once more the moonbeams were silvering the old oaks, and ere retiring to rest the brothers paced up and down under their shadows. The first to break the silence was the soldier one. " George," he said, "how shall I ever thank you and my mother for all the kindness you have shown my wife and child in my prolonged absence? All I can do is to pray God to bless and reward you. Many a night on the battlefield have I thanked God for the home so willingly offered by you to my young wife; and truly have you fulfilled your promise to act a brother's part to her."

" Nay," interrupted the laird, " say not a word more, Jack. Your wife has more than repaid us for any kindness shown to her. A very messenger from Heaven has she proved to me and mine. My children owe to her loving words and actions a new life. It was she who first told my little motherless Gretchen of a Saviour's love; she who opened my eyes to see how cruelly selfish I had been in my children's upbringing,—how little I was seeking to train them in the fear of God, or to carry out what I knew would have been the desire of their own mother as regarded them. She it was who led our old respected preceptor, Mr. Ross, to the cross of Jesus ; and it was her words of love and peace that touched the heart of my boy, and has given him the desire to consecrate his marvellous musical talents to the Lord. And Hannah, too—have you noticed the change in her, Jack? Well, by God's grace, it was Edith's life of love and patience that opened her heart ; and it was Edith's words about the love of Jesus that the Holy Spirit used to lead her to the Saviour ; and now she, in her own turn, is adorning in her daily walk the doctrines of Christ. Ay, and many more hearts have also, by God's grace, been ' won by love.' "

Colonel Ogilvie's voice was choked by emotion, as, after listening to these things, he strove to say, " Thank God ! " And all the while the old oaks, in their solemn grandeur, looked down on the two brothers ; and, as their branches gently waved to and fro, seemed, as Gretchen would have said, to give their assent to the truth of what the Laird of Oakwood had been telling of the blessing that Edith Ogilvie had proved to the inmates of the old castle.

One thing only seemed wanting to complete the happiness of all that evening, and that was the

presence of Max ; but that might not be.   The
lad was still away pursuing his musical education ;
but loving letters came from him from time to
time.   His powers were developing, and masters
of the art spoke of him in the highest terms.   But
his heart beat true to his loved ones, and very
specially to his sister Gretchen ; and sometimes he
would tell her, that much as he loved to hear the
music of the master composers around him, he
often longed once more to hear the strange, weird
music of the winter winds amid the branches of the
old oaks at Oakwood Castle.

It was the golden autumn time, when the earth
was yielding her rich store of grain and fruit, when
the old-fashioned carriage drove to the castle gate
to take Colonel Ogilvie with his wife and child to
the little town, to meet the stage-coach which was
to convey them to their English home, where, in a
few weeks, Gretchen was to join them.   The parting words were said amid many tears, and even
sobs were heard from the old servants, and Edith
Ogilvie drove off, followed by the blessings of
many hearts; and even James Duncan was heard to
say that the happiest event that had ever occurred
at the castle was the coming there of the young
bride, the ruling motive of whose life was " the
love of Christ constraining her."   " Ay, truly,"

GOLDEN CROWN LIBRARY

OF STORIES BY AUTHORS OF HIGH REPUTE

1 HERSELF AND HER BOY............Amy le Feuvre

3 HER HUSBAND'S HOME............E. Everett Green

4 PEPPER & CO.....................Esther E. Enock

5 ELDWYTH'S CHOICE...............L. A. Barter Snow

6 MARTYRLAND.....................Robert Simpson

7 ANDY MAN.......................Amy le Feuvre

9 FOUR GATES.....................Amy le Feuvre

10 URSULA ....L. A. Barter Snow

11 A MADCAP FAMILY...............Amy le Feuvre

12 NORAH'S VICTORY...............L. A. Barter Snow

13 JOAN'S HANDFUL................Amy le Feuvre

14 CORAL ....Charlotte Murray

15 SOME BUILDERS.................Amy le Feuvre

16 AGNES DEWSBURY................L. A. Barter Snow

17 MARGARET'S STORY..............Marjory Douglas

18 'TWIXT ALTAR AND PLOUGH......L. A. Barter Snow

19 TRUE TO THE LAST..............E. Everett Green

20 MY LADY'S GOLDEN FOOTSTEPS..E. E. Enock

21 NORAH: A GIRL OF GRIT.........Beth J. C. Harris

22 HER LITTLE KINGDOM............L. A. Barter Snow

23 BRAVE BROTHERS................E. M. Stooke

24 A COUNTRY CORNER..............Amy le Feuvre

25 THE HOME OF THE AYLMERS......Marjorie Douglas

Coloured Frontispiece
Crown Octavo 2/6 Net

Pickering
& Inglis